WORKING FOR A MOB BOSS
The Funny Detective – Volume 3

I0630425

David Berardelli

WORKING FOR A MOB BOSS
The Funny Detective – Volume 3

FICTION4ALL

Chapter One - Friday

At seven-thirty, my dead buddy Mike still hadn't come out of the ladies' room.

Once again I scanned the crowded restaurant to make sure she wasn't mingling. Not that a dead person could actually mingle or would even want to... but knowing Mike as I did, I wouldn't be surprised to see her doing anything.

Mike certainly had some strange ways. Last year, as I questioned one of my contacts in the St. Cloud Walmart, she'd wandered off to check out fabrics. Naturally, I didn't make an issue of it. I try very hard not to find fault with things Mike does. She helps me solve my cases and has saved my life several times in the two years we've been working together. In other words, I try not to question anything because I don't want her to get pissed off and disappear.

I gave the big candlelit room another quick glance and checked my watch again. Twenty minutes and still no sign of her.

What the hell could she be doing in there? Why would a spirit need to use the john? How could anyone perform bodily functions without a physical body?

This couldn't possibly be a bodily function type of thing. Maybe she wanted to check out the décor or give herself a once-over in the mirror. She wouldn't need twenty minutes for either task-- especially the once-over thing. Mike looked fabulous for a dead babe. Anyone who saw her wouldn't mind being dead if it meant looking as good as she did.

I finished my T-bone and scraped out the last of the soft, buttery innards of my baked potato. I still had about two inches of red wine left in my glass, so I figured ten minutes, tops, before I'd be leaving Charley's Steakhouse.

I'd just spent eight long hours waiting for two clients to call me back. Since the workday had ended without a single call, I decided to treat myself to a steak dinner as a reward for my perseverance. To top off the evening on a positive note, I planned on driving back to my place after dinner, opening a new bottle of Jack Daniel's, and watching a mindless scream flick on Netflix. When you find yourself without a date on a Friday night, you do whatever makes you happy. I thought I had a date in the works, but the confused lady in question had called this afternoon to tell me she'd decided to spend the weekend with her husband.

I've never been a big fan of threesomes.

I didn't want to leave Charley's without letting Mike know. That would be rude, and I didn't want to tick her off. She might not show up the next time I needed her. In my line of work, when your partner doesn't show at the right time, you could end up dead.

I couldn't ask my waitress to check on her. For one thing, Mike didn't let just anyone see her. When she did, it was for a really good reason. Letting your ectoplasm fly isn't as easy as it sounds. You have to concentrate, for one thing. And you can only sustain it for short periods.

I knew that if I asked our waitress to check on a woman who wasn't there to begin with, I'd probably be asked to leave and never come back. This was one of the few restaurants in the area that offered great food and great service, so I didn't want that to happen.

I couldn't help wondering if Mike was still miffed because I didn't tell her I was driving to Lauderdale to visit my mother last month. I hadn't wanted to take the trip in the first place, but Mom had been bugging me for some time to come down and see her, and since I hadn't had any cases in over a week, I decided to make the trip. I'd wanted to see her, I admit it. It had been a while since I'd taken time off.

That dreaded ritual of humiliation and degradation that always happens in Italian families engulfed me as soon as I pulled up Mom's short concrete drive and got out of my classic TransAm. Hugging. Kissing. Pinching. Cheek-squeezing. The circles around my eyes were closely examined and analyzed, followed by the obligatory and highly embarrassing stomach-pat--first by Mom, then Uncle Nicky, Aunt Rose, and Aunt Charlotte. Uncle Al, bless him, was the only one in the group who didn't overindulge himself. A firm handshake, followed by a quick hug and slap on the back of the head, and his ritual was complete.

My first of several required punishments was scheduled for the following afternoon. Mom informed me that I was to help Uncle Nicky with his shed project. Such a task doesn't normally sound particularly intimidating, but when the job involves a stubborn elderly Italian who'd spent his life doing carpentry work, any outside assistance immediately becomes an exercise in gross futility.

My only task was to transform my body into a living, breathing tool rack. For four hours that afternoon, I stood as silently as a department store dummy, gripping screwdrivers, hammers, nails and screws, while my uncle rambled on and on about the "good ol' days, when a fella worked all day long with his hands . . . and put his heart and soul into his work . . . and treated his tools with great reverence. They're your best friends. You treat 'em good, they'll treat you the same--*capire*?"

I nodded dutifully, agreeing with him whenever he paused during a long rant, and handing him whatever he dictated.

The following afternoon, I helped him lower a kitchen cabinet for Mom so she wouldn't have to use the stepstool to get to her condiments. For this assignment I was required to become a handy jack stand by resting the center of the heavy piece on my head while my uncle measured, drilled holes, and bolted the cabinet into the wall.

The next day, I was roped into taking Mom, Aunt Rose, and Aunt Charlotte to the local mall to help with their weekly grocery shopping. Little did I know that these women would spend the entire day checking out each and every clothing store, coffee shop, flower boutique, jewelry exchange, toy store

8

and antique shop in the huge complex. For this outing, I was required to carry all their purchases and was forced to make three separate trips to the parking lot to stuff everything into the trunk of Aunt Rose's Town Car.

Since they all considered me skinny and underfed, Mom, Aunt Rose and Aunt Charlotte filled me up with lasagna, ravioli, gnocchi, Italian bread, and Mom's homemade *biscotti*. I was soon bloated and gassy, waddling around like a pregnant hippo, popping Tums, and making hasty exits to the john so I wouldn't embarrass myself.

After three days with my relatives, I prayed for a swift and painless death--or some way of sneaking away and waddling back to Orlando, where my quiet, relative-free apartment hungrily awaited my return.

Then, in the midst of my anguish, Mike appeared in my bedroom the morning after my day at the Mall, as I was getting ready for breakfast. Quite naturally I was shocked, but relieved, as well. With Mike at my side for moral support, I should feel less intimidated by my relatives.

Sounded reasonable, didn't it?

But as I gave the situation some thought, my initial relief vanished. Mike could be extremely playful at times and often didn't realize the impact it had on me.

I spent the morning rather nervously, not knowing what she was going to do or when she was going to do it. I asked her a number of times to please behave--and not do anything that would embarrass me. She smiled and told me she'd be a good girl. However, the twinkle in her eyes told me otherwise.

She stood beside my chair in the kitchen, watching Mom at the stove, frying eggs.

"Your mom's very pretty."

I just smiled.

"You have her eyes."

I sighed and sipped my coffee.

"How is it?" Mike asked. "It smells heavenly."

"Coffee's perfect, Mom."

Mom just shrugged and flipped the bacon on the griddle. "I make it the same way all the time, Ralphie."

"It's really good. And don't call me Ralphie."

Mike asked if I'd introduce her.

I gave her one of my meaningful glares. She responded with a smile and said, "I know I'm not Catholic or Italian--at least I wasn't when I was alive--but maybe she'll like me anyway. I could act like a lady and cross my legs properly when I sit, if that'll help."

I groaned.

"I'll even tell her I'm a virgin. Will that help?"

I rubbed my eyes and focused on trying to act normal.

As soon as we were alone, I told Mike once again to cool it. If my mother even suspected I was communicating with someone from the Great Beyond, she'd get together with everyone in the family and haul me off to the nearest psychiatrist.

Or the neighborhood priest, to schedule an immediate exorcism.

Mike understood, of course, but I could tell she was having too much fun. She continued making comments and observations, but was careful to do it with more finesse, and limited it to moments when we were alone, or when Mom was busy in the kitchen with my aunts.

Even so, Mom picked up on my uneasiness. As with all old-fashioned Italian mothers, she blamed everything on my diet and my high-stressed job. "You need to find a different job, Ralphie," she said, shaking her long, slender index finger at me. "This silly cowboys-and-Indians foolishness is ruining your health."

"Cops and robbers, Mom. And don't call me Ralphie."

"I don't care what it's called. It's not good for you."

Thankfully, the visit ended without further incident. Even so, I couldn't get the TransAm on the road fast enough for the long drive back to Orlando.

My waitress came over to see how I was doing. Her nametag said *HI! I'M EVELYN*. She was about fifty, short and broad, sporting the tattoo of a small blue star on her left wrist and a yellow starfish on the back of her right hand. She wore a nose stud and ear studs, and her red hair was piled high, held in place with a blue scarf. Pens and pencils stuck out from the bun like colorful bird perches. I didn't know if she'd forgotten about them or wore them for decorative reasons. I wondered if anything else was wandering around in there.

"Get ya anything, honey?"

I resisted the urge to ask if she could make a quick trip to the ladies' room for me.

"I think that'll be it."

"No coffee?"

"I'm good, thanks."

She pulled out her pad and checked one of her pockets for something to write with. I wanted to grab one of the pencils jutting out of her bun. That would probably get me slapped. She found a pencil in her apron pocket, scribbled the amount of the tab and ripped it from the pad. She slid the scrap of paper carefully beneath my plate and told me to come back again real soon. As she whisked away, she stuck the pencil in her bun.

I pulled out a couple of twenties and tucked them in with the check. One last glance of the big candlelit room and still no sign. I knew not to worry. That would be silly. No one could see Mike. She couldn't be assaulted or mugged, and there was little chance of her being kidnapped at gunpoint. I wasn't afraid of leaving her here. She knew where I lived.

After all, she'd made it to my mother's place in Lauderdale without any trouble.

I climbed down the wooden porch steps that led to the front lot facing Michigan Avenue. I slid behind the wheel of my classic TransAm. It was a cool, clear night--typical for Central Florida in early spring. I fired up the sleeping monster and lowered the windows. I'd spent a fortune two months ago on a new compressor but hadn't been able to test it because of the cool early April weather. I'd had it done during the winter, hoping I could get a deal. The only "deal" I got was that they did a good job and hadn't encountered any other problems.

I pulled onto Michigan and drove east, toward Conway Road. Traffic was pretty heavy. On Friday night, everyone heads for the bars, the tourist traps, downtown, Disney, or South Orange Blossom Trail for the hookers and sleaze shops.

I got onto Conway and headed north.

Less than a mile later, I noticed someone following me.

***

If I ever took the time to sit down and write a manual of instructions for being a successful private eye, I'd include a section on how to lose a tail.

Being followed happens a lot in the detective business. When you stalk people, they get angry. And when people are angry, they do stupid things. One of them, naturally, involves stalking you back. In most cases, common sense dictates what procedure you should follow to handle such a situation. One simple procedure, I've learned, will give you a slight edge. Simply put: Don't let the guy following you know you're aware of him.

In such situations, most people aren't able to keep calm or think rationally. Panic sets in and they react stupidly. Their first reaction is to try and lose the tail. This will only cause more trouble. If the tail guy is a professional, he'll know exactly what you're trying to do and will easily counter every action you make. He might even try to ram your car or shoot out one of the tires. Your chances of losing him will evaporate. Even with Lady Luck on your side, it's extremely difficult to lose a tail in city traffic.

My personal method is to act totally clueless--a condition that has always come very naturally for me. This way, the tail guy will be caught totally unawares when I suddenly run a red light, or zip in front of the vehicle in the next lane.

In the detective business, you make more enemies than friends. Sure, when you solve a case, you make your client happy. Many times, your client is so happy that he even pays you for your services. If you're lucky, the check doesn't bounce, and you can keep him on your list of potential repeat customers. But he's not the one you have to worry about.

The gentleman you burned to solve the case is the one to lose sleep over. He's not happy at all. In most cases, he's downright miserable, and might even plan revenge. If he's got a screw loose--which describes most of the people I come into contact with--he'll want to get even and won't care how long it takes.

I had to assume that the guy following me was someone I'd burned in the past. I also had to assume he had a screw loose. Anyone out in heavy Friday night traffic who doesn't have to has definitely got a screw loose.

I opened my console and pulled out the Beretta Cheetah .380. I'd been using it for the last several years, alternating it with the Bersa .380, a cheaper but reliable gun made in Brazil. Both guns are compact, light, easy to handle, and pack a wallop. I don't usually carry a gun unless I'm on a case and expecting trouble. I didn't expect trouble when I drove to Charley's for that steak dinner.

I switched the gun off safety and laid it on top of the console. I hoped I wouldn't have to use it, but in this business, you never know. I'm not the world's greatest shot--I admit it. I really should spend a few afternoons at the shooting range whenever I get the chance, but I'm always embarrassed whenever I do go there. I usually hit the metal frame of the target retriever, causing a ricochet that nearly gets me or the poor guy in the next booth, or I nail the target in the next booth, pissing off whoever's there. Both incidents always make me want to evaporate into the floor tiles.

Hopefully I wouldn't need the gun tonight. If I could gain some distance, I could negotiate a quick turn-off and get off the main stretch. This would alert my tail, but short of pulling over and asking him his intentions, I didn't see any other option.

I began wondering once again why Mike had vanished at the restaurant. She'd wandered off before, of course, but usually gave me a heads-up. Tonight she hadn't said anything, just stared at the crowd as I ate my steak. She mentioned the ladies' room a few minutes later and got right up, heading off in that direction.

Dead or alive, women were impossible to figure.

But the fact remained--I needed Mike's help.

"Dammit, Mike," I yelled at the dark, empty cab, "where the hell did you go?"

"Sounds like someone really missed me."

I nearly swerved into the next lane at the sound of her voice. She'd materialized on the passenger's side, appearing in her red tee shirt, jeans, and silver necklace and bracelets. Her long chestnut hair spilled heavily over her shoulders.

"How could you tell?"

She shrugged. "You're wearing your mad face?"

"Can't help it. I'm upset."

"Why are you wearing your mad face?"

"What happened back at the restaurant? Why'd you just disappear?"

"I always come back, don't I?"

"I'm being tailed. And I thought I pissed you off."

"When did you piss me off? And who's tailing you?"

"At my mom's. And if I knew who was tailing me, I wouldn't be so upset."

"What happened at your mom's? I was just having fun. I thought you knew that."

"A guy thinks all sorts of weird things when he's nervous."

"Why are you nervous?"

"I just told you. I'm being followed."

"I just wanted to check out the ladies' room."

"It sure took you long enough."

"When I went in there, I bumped into another dead girl. Her name is Patty, and she's really pretty. She was standing in front of the mirror, feeling sorry for herself."

"Why?"

"She's dead, silly."

"Oh."

"Anyway, she's been having trouble coping. She hasn't been dead long, and hasn't learned how to do her ectoplasm right. It's kind of like getting the right shade of makeup--know what I mean? She likes to talk, and before I knew it, we were chatting away about so many things, I completely forgot about the time, and when I came back out, you'd already gone."

Jeez. I was not in the mood for all that. "Can we please talk about this later?"

"What would you like to talk about instead?"

I took a deep breath and waited for my blood pressure to go back down. "Um . . . the dude in the car behind us, for starters?"

She nodded. "The one following you?"

"That's the one."

"What is it about him you'd like to talk about?"

I groaned. Mike's playfulness sometimes wore thin on my nerves. This was one of those times. "How about why he's tailing me, for starters?"

"I don't know. I just got here."

"Can you please find out?"

"Sure thing. But only because you said please."

17

I waited for her to disappear, but she didn't budge.

"Something wrong?" I asked.

"Why do you ask?"

"You're still here."

"I'm waiting."

"For what?"

"A red light. You don't want me to fly around out there while everyone's zooming by so fast, do you? I might land in the wrong car. I might also hurt something. You wouldn't want me hurting anything, would you?"

"Mike. . ."

"Yes?"

A yellow light flickered not far straight ahead. I began slowing down.

"You know something, Mike? Sometimes I really wonder about you."

She'd already disappeared.

Chapter Two

The light changed.

I kept with the flow. As I crept up to the next intersection, I wanted to force the TransAm into a quick U-turn. That would be stupid. It wouldn't take Mike long to find out what was going on. I could wait.

I realized I could be totally wrong about all this. For all I knew, this could be my paranoia taking over. My imagination had a history of going all screwy when I had too much time on my hands and found myself in heavy traffic.

Heavy Central Florida traffic can turn the most laid-back driver into a whimpering idiot. Out-of-state tags, rental cars, tour buses and local traffic, all intent on reaching their destinations at the highest rate of speed, turn the highways into a suicidal maze. Toss in a large percentage of drunks and dope-heads on Friday and Saturday nights and you'll understand the nature of true paranoia.

I've lived in Orlando nearly all my life and should be used to heavy traffic. Congested highways became a staple in this neck of the woods ever since Disney set up shop in the early seventies. Being followed or tailgated should be second nature to me.

It would be, too--if I wasn't a detective.

Hopefully Mike would soon find out that my "tail" was actually an old woman returning from Bingo. Or a family of five on their way to Disney

Village to take in a light show. I knew Disney Village was in the opposite direction, but when you're trying to be optimistic, practicality flies right out the window.

I sure hoped this was the case. I wanted only to return to my apartment, open that bottle and indulge in a mindless scream fest. Regular glimpses of wet tee shirts and tanned female flesh would bring about a pleasant end to a long, unproductive day.

I stopped at the intersection and reminded myself once again to stay with the flow. The worst thing I could do was head home. If this *was* a tail, I didn't want the bad guy to know where I lived. If he was a professional, he already knew. I just didn't want to make his job easier by bringing him home with me. Sharing good whiskey with someone ordered to kill you is pretty stupid. And a waste of good whiskey.

"I'm back." Mike materialized beside me again.

"What kept you?"

"You're kidding, right?"

"Right. I'm kidding. What's going on?"

"I wish I knew."

"Didn't you see who's in the car?"

"Uh-huh. . ."

"Well?"

She shrugged. "They didn't say anything."

"They?"

"There are two guys."

So much for my little-old-lady-Bingo theory, as well as the Disney Village hunch.

The light changed, and I went straight. I wanted her to say she thought the two men were harmless. Her silence didn't make me feel any better.

"They didn't say anything?"

"Not a thing. It was kind of boring in there. I was tempted to ask them if they were following you, but I didn't think that would go over too well."

This told me the worst. Mob guys didn't speak much, especially on a job. But I couldn't automatically assume they were mob hitters just because they weren't chattering away.

"Can you give me a description?"

"It was dark in there."

"Try anyway."

"Okay. They were both guys . . ."

"You already said that."

"Did I say they were big? They were also broad-shouldered. And dark."

"Dark?"

"Dark hair and eyes. The driver has a mustache. The passenger has one eyebrow."

"Over which eye?"

"Both."

This was beginning to sound very mobbish. But I couldn't panic just yet. There were other nationalities besides Italians who had one eyebrow. "Anything else?"

"Not really. Just that they had guns."

I swerved, my tires bumping the curb. "Guns?"

"Those ugly black metal things with a trigger and bullets--"

"What I meant was, how do you know?"

21

"I smelled it."

"Smelled what?"

"The powder. What do you call it?"

"Gun powder."

"I was thinking of something else, smarty."

"Cordite?"

"That's it."

"I didn't realize your smeller was so good."

"A lot of things have gotten better since I died. Weird, huh?"

The two might have recently fired their weapons. This, of course, edged my paranoia a few notches closer to the suffocating level.

"I wouldn't worry too much about any of this," she said.

I couldn't believe she'd just said that. "You just said there are two of them."

"Right."

"You also said they have guns."

"Yes . . ."

"You smelled cordite--which could mean they might have fired them recently."

"That makes sense."

"So now I'd like you to tell me why I shouldn't worry."

She smiled. "You have *me* on your side, silly boy."

***

I pulled into a shopping plaza on East Michigan, about a mile west of South Conway.

At the far end of the long building, a square sign flashing *DRINKS 4 U* in bright neon lit up the parking lot. At this time of night, few of the other stores were still open. Most of the parked vehicles sat in the general vicinity of the bar.

A crowded bar can be your best friend when people are after you. If you know the barman, manager, or even one or two of the customers, you'll be noticed. Even if you don't know anyone, it's much more difficult to be grabbed and dragged outside when you're amongst a bunch of people. Even drunk, people tend to notice such things.

"Drinks for you?" Mike was frowning.

"It's a *bar*, baby. With *drinks*. Get it?"

"It's a tacky name. Not much better than *EATS*."

"I didn't know you were such a snob."

"I'm *so* not a snob. Did you forget where we first met?"

"In the men's room at one of the worst dives in Orlando. Of course I didn't forget."

"How could you accuse me of such a thing, then?"

"Who else but a snob would condemn a place just because of its name?"

She shrugged. "Can't help it. It sounds brainless. Like the owner couldn't think of something better."

"What's in a name, anyway? We have different things to worry about."

My tail car had pulled into a space about ten spots down, doused its lights and just sat there.

My pulse hammered wildly. I half-expected them to get out and walk right over. I also expected them to have their guns out as they approached. I even expected to see one of them carrying a sack to stuff me into. Or a pillowcase for my head. Kidnappers always seem to have a pillowcase handy when they're looking for a victim.

"No one's getting out," I said.

"They're probably waiting to see what you plan to do."

"You're probably right."

"What's your plan?"

"I thought I'd just stroll into the bar for a drink."

"Then what?"

"Maybe talk to the barman about basketball. Or football."

"You're not even a sports guy."

"I know. I hate jocks. They used to do disgusting things to me in high school."

"Then why would you--"

"If I'm talking to someone, those boys won't be able to grab me. The barman's always the best guy to talk to. Even when he doesn't talk, he listens. And he notices everything."

"And if the barman's talking to someone else? What if he's in the john when you walk in?"

"Why do you always have to mess up my plans?"

"I'm only saying you should be prepared for anything."

"When I'm scared, my brain doesn't work as well as it should."

"You're a private eye."

24

"So? We're also human. We're allowed to get scared, too."

"Private eyes face more danger and stressful situations than the average person."

"Your point?"

"Private eyes should be able to function much more efficiently than normal people under adverse conditions."

"Bull crap."

"You really think so?"

"Not really . . ."

"Why say it, then?"

"Just trying to slip in a little bravado among my shaking chicken bones."

"I understand. Here's something else to consider. What happens if you don't make it inside?"

"How's that?"

"What if they stop you before you reach the door?"

I was right. That hadn't occurred to me. And it should have; they were parked closer to the door than I was. "Got any ideas?"

"Maybe . . ."

I waited, but she said nothing. "If you're expecting a drum roll, I left my drumsticks back at the apartment with my harmonica."

"I'd rather show you."

"Is this a magic trick? Do I need a hat? Would a baseball cap do?"

"Just get out of the car and head on over to the building. Walk fairly fast, and try not to let them grab you."

"And then?"

"I'll show you my magic trick."

"Can't you just tell me?"

Her smile told me she was having entirely too much fun. One day I'd have to remind her that mortals took things like this more seriously than spirits obviously did.

"I guess I don't have much choice, do I?"

"Nope."

"Then I'd better just shut up and do what I'm told."

"Good choice." She disappeared.

I briefly considered taking the .380. If those two were pros, they could get to their guns much faster than me and were probably much better shots than I was.

I opened the console and put the gun inside. My hand shook as I pulled the keys from the ignition and pushed open the door.

***

The two men caught up to me before I made it halfway to the building.

Mike had been right. They were big, both at least half a head taller than me, and broad at the shoulders. The driver probably went an easy two-seventy, his partner two-forty or so. Even so, they moved with cat-like grace, slipping silently out of the dark sedan and coming at me with calculated precision.

They could be bouncers from one of the strip clubs on the Trail. They were as big as the ones I'd seen, but older. The driver was about forty, his partner a few years younger. The passenger was the one blocking my way back to the TransAm. The driver had veered left, blocking my passage to the bar. I backed up so I could watch both of them, but they'd moved in closer, like lions circling their prey just before the kill, until they were both less than ten feet away. The maneuver was done flawlessly, in perfect sync. They'd obviously done this before.

I hoped Mike wasn't far. I couldn't wait to see her magic trick.

Meanwhile, I had to stall them.

"What's going on, guys? This wouldn't happen to be a mugging, would it?" I was surprised my voice even worked. "If so, I would've brought along some cash."

The driver pointed to their ride. He obviously wanted me to get in.

I had no intention of making this easy for them, so I acted stupid and naïve--two things that had always been second nature for me.

I nodded approvingly. "Nice ride. Looks like a Challenger. New model, too. I'll bet she flies. But I'd put my TransAm up against her any day of the week. Maybe we can get on the GreeneWay and find out who's *really* got the monster machine."

Neither replied.

"I guess I need to ask again. What can I do for you two gentlemen? You want money? Or did you just come over to ask me to approve of your ride?"

Unibrow said, "Papa Joe wants to talk to you."

A whiff of wrongness drifted over, souring the cool night air.

Papa Joe Raguzzo had never contacted me this way before. Whenever he'd wanted to talk to me in the past, he'd called me on my cell. And his men never used his name in public.

These two had a mob look, but that didn't mean they worked for Papa Joe. The Raguzzo organization wasn't the only mob in Central Florida. With the drug cartels moving in from Mexico, South America and the Caribbean, Papa Joe had been having a difficult time maintaining his seniority. If he hadn't already snatched up the local strip club and porn industries, and kept up with his political connections, he'd be in serious trouble.

These guys looked more Hispanic than Italian, although Unibrow definitely had some black in his genes. The kinky hair and low slab-like forehead sealed the deal. But none of this told me anything I needed to know. The only thing I cared about was how quickly they'd surrounded me. This suggested experience and training. They were obviously acting under orders, but just whose was anyone's guess.

It really didn't matter. They wanted me in their car. That was the part I didn't like.

But I couldn't let them take me without a fight.

"Did he tell you what this is all about?" I asked.

"Papa Joe . . . he don't tell us the details," the driver said.

"He just said find you and pick you up," Unibrow added.

28

They were both talking to keep me off-balance. I couldn't keep both of them in my sights without letting them get closer. I kept my position so I could see the driver, glancing at Unibrow every now and then as well.

"Papa Joe usually calls me when he wants to talk," I said. "What's wrong? His cell need a recharge?"

"He just said find you and bring you in," Unibrow repeated. He was getting anxious. His brow twitched in the center, and a vertical crack appeared, climbing up his forehead.

"Right now?"

The driver nodded.

"On a Friday night?"

The driver nodded again.

"At this time of night?"

"C'mon." Unibrow gestured.

"And if I say I'd rather call Papa Joe myself and see what he wants, instead of dropping in on him on a Friday night, when he's usually at his mansion with his wife Roslyn and the rest of the family?"

The driver reached into his jacket pocket. So did Unibrow.

I'd just run out of options.

"Hey, baby! Whaddya doin' over there?"

Mike's voice issued loudly from a small cluster of parked vehicles sitting to my left. It sounded like it had come from the white Vette parked beside the black SUV, but with the shifting of the night air, it might have come from one of the fancy pickups half a dozen spots down.

Both had stiffened at the sound of her voice. The driver backed up and gawked in her direction. Unibrow's jaw dropped. So did their gun hands.

"Why haven't you come over to talk to me?" she called. "I told you which car my husband lets me drive when he's out of town. I've been waiting here nearly twenty minutes. You told me you wouldn't be late this time. Know how many guys have hit on me on their way inside?"

"Um, five?"

"Try ten. Two of them even looked prosperous. Who're those guys?"

"They didn't give me their names."

"What do they want? Don't tell me they're friends of yours. . ."

"I've never seen them before."

"Then ask them what they want. I'm horny and want to get out of here. This place is giving me the creeps."

"They want me to get in the car with them."

"Listen, baby . . . I'll give you two minutes to get rid of them. Otherwise, I'm gone."

I shrugged. "C'mon, guys. Give me a break, okay?" I lowered my voice. "This lady's hot. I mean *smoldering*."

"What exactly do you want with my date?" she called. "You're not funny, are ya?"

The driver took another step back and frowned at his partner.

"Listen . . . I'm havin' a party for my guy here. We're going to my place to celebrate. It's his fortieth birthday. You wanna come, too? I guess it'll be all right. As they say, the more the merrier. But whatever you wanna do, let's do it. Like I said, I'm getting seriously horny."

"C'mon," the driver muttered.

Both bolted back to the sedan.

"You'll be hearing from us again," the driver said, and squeezed carefully behind the wheel.

The sedan fired up and roared out of there.

I tried getting a tag number but part of it had been smeared with mud. Obviously stolen.

"How'd I do?" Mike's voice asked, growing closer. She continued to remain invisible.

"Why must you advertise my age? I only turned forty a couple of months ago."

"Last November."

"Whatever."

"Anyway, what's it matter? I think you look great for your age. Very distinguished."

"That *really* makes me feel old."

"Oh, you're not old at all. Now please tell me how I did."

"If you hadn't mentioned my age, I'd consider that piece of work a study of true genius."

"I guess that means I did good, then. . ."

"You did. Now please stop telling people my age."

"I'll try."

Chapter Three

We got back to my South Conway apartment complex a little after nine.

Most of the tenants are elderly, which suits me. A relaxed atmosphere hits the spot after a hard day-- especially when you've just been followed through town by two mob guys intent on tossing you in their car. Aside from weekly ambulance visits from ORMC and afternoon bingo in the rec room beside the pool, the complex doesn't see much activity. Elderly people tend to stick together. Any stranger foolish enough to park in someone's assigned space stands a good chance of being surrounded by a gang of feisty geriatric residents demanding an explanation.

Tonight, scattered groups of oldsters in loose-fitting jogging apparel shuffled around the complex. The lighted tennis court was deserted. Laughter resonated from the pool area, where visiting relatives from the north frolicked in the chilly chlorinated water.

I saw no suspicious vehicles across the aisle or near my building. The dark-colored Challenger was nowhere in sight. If someone was lurking in the shadows, Mike would have no trouble sniffing them out.

I parked in my designated space, doused the lights and flicked off the engine. Before getting out, I gave the area one last scan.

I crossed the street and stopped at the edge of the front stoop, about ten feet from the door. My nerves still twitched from the encounter outside the bar. I'd just escaped a bad situation but remained in defensive mode. In my view, standing in front of a door or window right now begged for trouble. "Mike?" I whispered at the hazy darkness.

"Right here," she replied a couple of feet away, on my right.

"Anyone inside?"

"I can't see from here."

I groaned. "You might want to shift your position a little, if it's not too much trouble."

"No problem." Silence for about five seconds. Then: "No one there."

It amazed me how quick she was. Even so, I didn't want to take chances. "How about my bedroom?"

"It's still there."

I rubbed my temples. "I *meant*, did you check it?"

"Yep."

"Under the bed?"

"Nothing but a group of dust bunnies."

"Bedroom closet?"

"*Affirmativo*."

"Hall closet?"

"*Si*."

"Kitchen cabinet?"

"Nothing in there but cleaning stuff and a really gross-looking roach motel you should've tossed out months ago."

"I guess it was packed, then?"

"I didn't have time to check, smarty. You're in such a hurry tonight . . ."

I moved closer to the door. With shaky fingers I managed to slip the key into the slot and unlock the door. As soon as I pushed it open, I rushed inside and slammed it shut, deadlocking and chaining it immediately.

"I won't take offense that you just slammed the door in my face," Mike said behind me.

Without replying, I marched straight to the kitchen cabinet and grabbed the unopened bottle of Jack. My fingers still wouldn't work right, so I put the bottle on the counter, took the .380 out of my pants pocket and placed it on the counter next to the bottle. I took a few deep breaths to steady myself.

"I'd open it for you if I could." Mike materialized in the kitchen doorway. She'd changed into a sleeveless blue tee shirt, tan Capri's and tennies. She must have done it only moments ago.

"Why'd you change?"

"You don't like this outfit?"

"I don't remember saying that."

"You didn't."

"Then why assume that's what I meant?"

"Because men don't usually notice stuff unless there's a reason."

"I'm a detective. I notice a lot of things."

"So you do like this one?"

"You could say that."

"But not the other one?"

"I like the other one, too."

34

"Which do you like better?"

I just sighed.

"Don't tell me you've forgotten already. . ."

"It was a red tee shirt, jeans and pumps."

"You really did notice."

"Of course I noticed, dammit."

"Now you're angry again."

"Just frustrated."

"But not angry?"

"Maybe a little."

"Good. Think you can open that bottle now?"

I twisted it open like a champ. My fingers had gone right back to being functional. It was amazing how a woman could manipulate a guy, even when she was dead. I snatched a clean glass from the drainer and poured it a quarter full. "How about that? I can even handle a glass without dropping it."

"I'm *so* proud of you." Mike drifted over to my stereo and studied the stack of jazz CDs on top of the walnut cabinet. "What do we do now?" she asked. "We got rid of them, but I can't guarantee they'll stay away. Think they know where you live?"

I drank some Jack and let the fiery whiskey warm my insides. "If they're mob guys, they know where I live. And if someone has a contract on me, it won't be long before they try again. Since those two failed, it'll probably be someone else the next time."

"Why would anyone want you dead?"

I smiled. "You're sweet."

"I mean it. You're a really nice guy. A little crazy, sometimes, but you don't go out of your way to hurt people. You try to help them. I know you do it for money, but I think you do it because you're a good person. That's how we met just before I died--remember?"

"Of course."

"So why would someone want you dead?"

"I go after bad guys and get them in trouble. When someone's burned, they go after me. Sometimes they even manage to catch me. This happens a lot in the profession--which is one of the main reasons why my wife left me."

"Just *one* of them?"

"She also got tired of driving to the Emergency Ward to see if I was still alive."

"I can understand why she left."

"You women. You're always sticking together."

"It's an estrogen thing."

"I knew it was something silly."

She sighed. "Anyway, you don't think those two are working for that mob guy friend of yours, do you?"

"Raguzzo's not what you'd call my friend. I think he's still spooked over that car bomb you found under the TransAm at the Florida Mall two years ago. Mob guys respect that kind of efficiency. They also like it when someone gives them a heads-up, as we did last year."

"If we did him that favor, he shouldn't send anyone after you, right?"

"I should be in pretty good standing with him. He's fairly honest for a mob boss. I can't see him double-crossing me."

"So how do you know who those two were?"

"I don't. But I've got to find out."

"How?"

"By calling Papa Joe and asking him what's going on."

"Think he knows?"

"I'm not sure, but there's one way to find out." After finishing my drink, I squeezed my cell out of my pants pocket.

"Know his number?"

"Only his closest friends have it. Besides, he's always changing it."

"Why?"

"Why do you think? He's paranoid." I dialed the number.

"Vesper's," a husky feminine voice said softly in my ear. "How may I help you?"

"I'd like to talk to Sonny."

Sonny Bergman had been managing Vesper's for several years. He'd come up from Miami about ten years ago to manage one of Papa Joe's Tampa clubs and did so well that Papa Joe had invited him to Orlando to manage Vesper's, which many considered Raguzzo's favorite and most successful club.

"May I ask who's calling?"

"Tell him Deacon."

"Last name?"

"Deacon."

"First name?"

"My mother never gave me one."

"One moment, Mr. Deacon."

Click.

I poured more Jack into my glass, went back into the living room and sat down on the couch. Mike remained near the stereo, studying my jazz collection. She'd faded a little but was still visible. I never tired of staring at her shapely ass. Even blurry, it looked fantastic.

"I wish I could play one of these," she said. "I can flick it on, but I can't very well take a CD out of the case and pop it into the player."

"What would you like to hear?"

"I've always liked Doc Severinsen. I like Miles Davis, too."

"If I don't have to go back out tonight, I'll put on something for you."

"Thank you. And *please* quit staring at my butt."

"Can't help it. It's really nice."

"Thank you. But stop doing it anyway."

"I thought you liked me doing it."

"Sometimes it's distracting."

"Okay. I'll try, but--"

"Whaddya want, Deacon?" Sonny's loud, abrasive voice made my eardrum crackle like a loose battery cable.

"Hi, Sonny." I switched ears. "How's business?"

"Busy, Deacon. That means you got about ten seconds to tell me why you're botherin' me on a Friday night."

"I need to talk to Papa Joe."

"Listen, Deacon . . . I know you and the boss got somethin' goin', and I gotta go along with it. But it's like this--"

"Two guys tried picking me up earlier tonight."

A pause. "I didn't know ya went that way, Deacon."

I wasn't in the mood for humor--especially from a gorilla with an attitude and custom-fitted imported suits. "It wasn't a sex thing, dammit. It was a kidnapping. You know. I got a gun in my pocket, get in the car, asshole. Something you might've seen firsthand, once or twice--before turning respectable, of course."

"Careful, now. You don't wanna hurt my feelings. I might hang up on ya."

"Wouldn't want that, would we?"

"Cut the shit. This happen outside Vesper's?"

"A bar just off East Michigan."

"And this concerns the boss how?"

"They said they were working for Papa Joe, and he wanted to talk to me. They were really eager to get me in their car."

Silence. I'd got him thinking. In Sonny's case, this wasn't an easy thing to do.

"I know your boss doesn't work that way, so I didn't go with them."

"They *letcha* go?"

"I slipped away when they weren't looking."

39

"They weren't our people, then."

"I didn't think they were."

"They were ours, ya wouldn'ta got away."

"Thanks for the spontaneous chest-thump, but that's not exactly what I need right now. Talk to him, okay?"

"He ain't here."

"I didn't think he would be. But let him know, all right? If someone's driving around, giving out your boss's name, this can't turn out well for any of us."

"I'll see what I can do." *Click*.

I finished my drink, got up and went over to the stereo. I picked up one of Doc's Command Performance CDs and slipped it into the player. By the time I turned it on, my cell buzzed.

"Figures," Mike said, just as Doc's soft, haunting trumpet began playing "*Stormy Weather*."

I put the volume on medium and took the cell down the hall so I could talk and let Mike enjoy the CD. I checked the display. *Unknown Name, Unknown Number*. Hopefully it was Papa Joe--not one of those telemarketers that liked catching people off-guard by calling late at night.

"Deacon here."

"What's this shit about you bothering Sonny Boy while he's trying to run my club?" The familiar gravelly Robert Loggia voice sounded more agitated than usual.

"Didn't he tell you?"

"This line bugged?"

"You know me better than that."

"Gotta ask."

"What did Sonny say?"

"He told me a coupla *sfachims* tried a snatch job on you. That about it?"

"They also mentioned your name several times."

"Bullshit. My people, they know better."

"I know."

"I no put no contract on you. You oughta know that."

"So glad to hear it."

"We're *paisanos*. We'll be even better *paisanos* if you quit bugging me and my associates."

"I didn't intend to bug you, but when two steroid freaks chase me through town and strongly suggest I climb in their car, it changes a guy's plans for the evening."

"I know nothing about any of this."

"I could tell this wasn't your way of doing things. How can we share a nice candlelight supper at your ridiculously-expensive restaurant if I'm dead?"

"Cut the bullshit. I already told ya, my place ain't that pricey. But it don't matter. It'll be on my tab, so why the fuck you keep bitching about my prices?"

"It's just my usual good-natured charm."

"You're a smartass. But like I said, those *stronzoni* ain't mine. I gotta find out about this."

"Please do. They're liable to come back any time and finish me off."

"Tell ya what. I'll have one of my boys come out and pick you up. He'll bring you to Dante's, we'll have some *vino*, and you can tell me all about those two."

"How will I know it's your boy and not someone else who wants me dead?"

"Ask him his momma's name."

"Who? The chauffer?"

"Of course, the fucking chauffeur! Who else we talking about?"

"How am I supposed to know the chauffeur's mother's name?"

"*Imbecille*. Pick a name, dammit."

"Okay. I get it. How about George?"

"You want his momma's name to be George?"

"I can't think of anything else right now. If he doesn't like it, ask him to pick one himself."

"*Idiota*. This is a fucking password. Just to make you feel better."

"Gotcha."

"You at your place?"

"I'll be sitting on my couch, drinking Jack Daniel's."

"I got better stuff at my place. Give him half an hour."

"I'll be here."

"Oh . . . and Deacon?"

"Still here."

"Leave the piece this time, *capire*?"

"If you insist."

"You'd better fucking believe I insist!"

***

Precisely thirty minutes later, my doorbell buzzed.

I grabbed the .380 and aimed it at the door.

Mike drifted over and stuck her head through the door for a quick peek outside. "It's a big guy in a chauffeur's uniform," she said, pulling her head back inside.

I killed the volume on Doc Severinsen's wild, big-band arrangement of "*Yesterdays*" and flicked off the CD player. "Is there a limo out there?"

She nodded.

I remained skeptical. A chauffeur's uniform and a limousine were convincing, but when your life's in danger, you tend not to trust the obvious. "How many brows does this guy have?"

"He's not one of them."

"How can you tell?"

"I don't know for sure. He just looks legit. And he's alone."

"You mean no one's with him?"

"You could say that."

"I guess I'm just jumpy."

"I don't blame you."

"I almost got kidnapped tonight."

"I know."

"At gunpoint."

"I was there, remember?"

I didn't say anything. I was too busy trying to figure out what I should do.

"Aren't you going to answer the door? If he tries something, I'll scare him."

She hadn't meant to make me feel like a moron, but I felt like one anyway. I was a grown man, a professional private eye . . . and suddenly afraid of opening my front door.

Man up, for God's sake. If he's a bad guy, shoot him.

I unlocked the door but kept the chain on. I held the gun against my right side, eased the door open and kept my right foot in its path, in case my visitor tried to force his way in. "Yes?"

"Mr. Deacon?" The man was big, broad-shouldered, and around thirty-five. His brows were black and thick, like a pair of healthy caterpillars. He was clean-shaven. I couldn't see his hair beneath his hat, but the sides were black and neatly trimmed.

Still not a hundred percent convinced, I didn't move.

"My employer wants me to pick you up."

My employer. That was reassuring.

"Okay. Just give me a minute."

The man blinked. "Aren't you supposed to ask me something first?"

Damn. I'd been so upset, I'd forgotten about that silly password thingy. *What the hell am I supposed to--*

"Ask him his mother's name," Mike whispered.

Yes! That was it.

"Um, what's your mother's name?"

"George."

Relief rippled down my limbs. "I'll be right there. Give me a minute."

"Mr. Deacon?"

"Yes?"

"Please leave your gun."

"No problem."

"You'll be patted down later on."

"I know."

"My employer will be extremely upset with both of us if you're carrying."

I closed the door, went over to the couch, and slid the gun beneath one of the cushions.

"Am I coming, too?" Mike had faded a little more.

"Do you want to?"

"I'll need to recharge. I'll be right there with you, but it'll be a little while before I can communicate with you."

"Just don't wander off, okay? I'll be with a mob boss on his turf, and I'll be unarmed. He says nothing can happen to me while I'm with him, but after what happened earlier, nothing can make me feel warm and cozy."

Chapter Four

Dante's *Ristorante*, with its trimmed gardens, sparkling fountain, and Italian-style courtyard, graced the elite Park Avenue district of Winter Park, eclipsing the neighboring shops, cafes, and markets in an area well-known for its panache.

The chauffeur dropped me off in front of the huge white stucco building. As soon as I went through the glass doors, two large men in tailored suits politely escorted me to the cloakroom, out of sight of the foyer. I held my arms straight out and made no threatening moves as the two men quickly and efficiently patted me down. After about twenty seconds, they both straightened and gave each other that silent exchange of approval only mob guys and battlefield comrades seem to understand.

Without a word, they led me back out into the foyer.

At nearly ten o'clock, the room was still moderately busy. The kitchen was in the process of closing up for the night, but succulent aromas of *sautéed* shrimp, charbroiled beef and freshly baked garlic bread clung stubbornly to the air. Even in my present state of paranoia, I found myself drooling as I eyed the plates on the tables I passed. It had been only a couple of hours since my steak dinner, but the smells overwhelmed me.

I had to stay focused. Earlier, I was almost kidnapped. A private detective learns to expect things like that, but it's still a big deal. I'd been kidnapped a few times before. I'd survived, but that didn't make the memories any better. In this case, I had to find out why it happened and who did it. Otherwise, I expected it to happen again.

Papa Joe sat in his usual booth at the far end of the big room, about ten feet down from the swinging doors leading to the kitchen. One of his men stood off to the side, just a few feet away, watching me. He was slightly smaller than the two who'd frisked me but just as formidable looking. His shoulders appeared cramped in the black suit. His arms hung loosely at his sides. He scanned the room while watching me at the same time. Thugs who could multitask impressed me.

Papa Joe wore a light-gray sport jacket with a white rose in his lapel, and a black shirt opened at the neck. He was sipping something from a small glass. A squat bottle of a golden liquid sat near his right elbow. He wore his ebony pinky ring and Rolex, and his nails were manicured and buffed. His leathery Robert Loggia-like face was tense and slightly pale, making him appear older. There was no humor or hint of friendliness in his features. The tight set of his sagging jawline, as well as the gray pouches beneath his small dark eyes, displayed his agitation. I couldn't blame him. He was probably enjoying a quiet evening with his family when Sonny buzzed him. He patted the space on his left as I approached. "Sit."

I sat.

He poured two inches of the golden stuff into the empty glass beside his own and carefully slid it over. "Drink. It's good stuff. Eighty years old, made in France. The French are pompous assholes, but they make good cognac."

I stared at the drink. The Jack Daniel's I'd had back at the apartment had already vanished from my system. I didn't care for cognac, but I needed something to settle my nerves. My suspicions, however, kept me from reaching for the glass. Someone tails me and mentions this man's name to get me in the car. I call this man, he brings me here, and now he wants me to drink something that looks like hamburger grease. He's obviously drinking the same thing, but I'm still suspicious, and my imagination is running on all eight cylinders.

"C'mon, *paisano*." His eyes were burning coals. "You no trust me at this stage?"

He was right. If he'd wanted me dead, I'd already be dead. I picked up the glass and coaxed a teaspoonful between my lips. It burned like hell, scalding my tongue, the roof of my mouth and the opening of my throat, heating up my insides even before it reached my gut.

Papa Joe's thick black brows slid up half an inch. He obviously wanted my opinion.

"It's a little like drinking flame," I said, and coughed.

Papa Joe nodded. He raised his right hand, and the guy with the cumbersome shoulders moved away.

Strange. I'd never known Papa Joe to shoo away his guards. Something was going on.

He moved closer, until the fumes of his aftershave singed the hair in my nostrils. "Tell me everything that happened tonight."

I told him.

He sat silently, digesting every word. Once I'd finished, he said, "One of them was black?"

"Kinky hair, low, slab-like forehead. He also had a unibrow."

"You said they were both around forty."

"The driver. The other guy was a few years younger."

"And they said my name?"

"Several times."

"If they were doing a hit, they wouldn'ta let you off. How'd you get away?"

I had to give him something believable, but it couldn't sound hokey. Raguzzo was a smart man, and difficult to deceive. He watched a man's eyes and body language and could easily tell what was going on. It was necessary for a man in his position to have this ability.

"Tell him about me," Mike whispered in my left ear. "Just don't tell him I'm dead."

"Something wrong?" he asked.

"Huh?"

"You tensed up."

"I'm still . . . nervous."

"Have more cognac. It's good for you."

"I don't want to get drunk."

His brows bumped together. "You're *Italiano*."

"What's that have to do with anything?"

"*Italianos* can drink. It should take more than a swallow of that stuff to get you plastered. Besides, didn't you tell me your old man was Irish?"

"Good point." I sipped more cognac. Despite my frayed nerves and scalded tongue, I found myself growing more relaxed.

"So . . . how'd you lose those *sfachims*?"

"I told you I was outside a bar."

"Yeah. Why'd you do that?"

"Do what?"

"Go to a bar when you were being followed."

"Safety in numbers."

Papa Joe nodded.

"Anyway, this beautiful babe came out of the bar just as the two were about to pull guns on me."

"Babe, eh?"

"A real sweet number."

"Thank you," Mike whispered.

"Blonde?"

"Brunette. She had beautiful dark brown hair and the most sensational almond eyes you'd ever want to see--"

"Oh, stop."

"She sounds nice." Papa Joe winked.

"Better than nice. Way better. In fact--"

"*Please* stop embarrassing me. . ."

"What did this beautiful lady do when she came outside?"

"She walked right over and started talking to me."

Papa Joe tilted his head. "Trying to hit on you?"

"She thought she knew me. High school, she said. Anyway, she came right over, and the two guys were so confused and surprised, they ran back to their car and drove off."

"They say anything?"

"The driver said this wasn't over."

Papa Joe nodded. "What about this babe?"

"She kind of figured I wasn't the guy she remembered, so she just went over to her car and drove away, too."

"Shame."

"I know. I would've loved to--"

"Watch it," Mike warned.

"I hear ya. If I was younger and didn't have a wife and family, I'd feel the same. But my Rosie, she's my lady. Nearly fifty years, now." Papa Joe finished his cognac, picked up the bottle and dropped another two inches into the glass. He gestured to my glass, but I shook my head. He put down the bottle, picked up his glass and raised it. "Rafaello, that lady prob'ly saved your life."

"Don't I know it. If she were here right now, I'd definitely want to, you know--"

"I said, *watch* it."

"Thank her properly. And by the way, drop the Rafaello. I prefer Deacon." I picked up my glass.

He frowned. "Yeah, I remember you're ashamed of your Italian name. These younger generations, they no have no respect for their roots." He sat back and stared straight ahead at the table of six people enjoying their *sautéed* shrimp dinner.

Something was definitely bothering him. Papa Joe wasn't normally this pensive. Or quiet.

I tried a gamble. "You know what this is all about, don't you?"

He stared at me. Fear, anger, and distrust showed clearly in the veiny black eyes. After an uncomfortable silence, he nodded.

"Care to tell me why you shooed away your bodyguard?"

He just sighed.

I was right. This was serious.

"There's something I need to know, and I'd like it if you told me right now, before we discuss anything else."

The dark burning coals flashed again. "Spit it out."

"Any idea why they were after me?"

"I can only guess."

"Tell me, then."

He finished his cognac and stared at the empty glass. He then shifted on the bench seat and stared at me. The burning coals had turned soft and liquid. They had difficulty staying on me, wanting to lower, to look inward. To hide. "I . . . was gonna hire you."

I didn't know if I should laugh or wait for a punch line. The same man who'd tried to have me killed wanted to hire me. Now I'd heard everything. To celebrate this milestone, I grabbed my glass and very carefully nudged a small drop of the corrosive acid over my lower lip, keeping my tongue out of the way to avoid another scalding. The potent liquid burned my mouth anyway.

I coughed and cleared my throat. I put the glass back down and promised my tongue and throat I would never again subject them to such blazing agony. "Hire me? For what?"

He went back to staring at his glass, then at the half-crowded room. "Somebody's trying to take over." His voice had become a hoarse whisper.

"The organization?"

His nod was slight, almost nonexistent.

Damn. I'd suspected something like this would happen. It's inevitable in such a dangerous, competitive business. However, I hadn't expected it to happen now. Papa Joe was still a strong, effective leader. "You're positive?"

A nod.

"And you want to hire me because . . . ?"

"Two reasons. First of all, I trust you."

I waited for him to say more. He went back to staring at his glass, the room, the cognac bottle. Then me. Deciding what to say next, what not to say. If he'd said too much.

This told me a lot. But I had to hear it from him before I could draw my own conclusions.

"Does the second reason have anything to do with why you just got rid of the guy with the shoulders?"

Another nod.

Now I knew the whole story.

Papa Joe couldn't trust anyone in his own organization.

***

53

I suddenly wanted to be somewhere else. The apartment. A movie theater. Another restaurant. Maybe one of the local bars.

Papa Joe was about to spill his guts, but I didn't want to sit here and listen.

I couldn't help the way I felt. Papa Joe was one of the most powerful men I knew. The city's mob boss. He knew important, successful people, ran most of the high-class hookers and porn shops in Central Florida, and also handled the largest part of the drug trade. He knew just about everything that was going on, and when someone caused problems, he made a phone call and the problem ceased being a problem.

But since he was now in trouble himself, he realized that he couldn't make that phone call. He couldn't trust anyone any longer. He wanted me to help him, but I had no idea if or how I could. Or even if I wanted to.

"Ask him what's going on," Mike urged. "And relax. You're acting like you're on a bad blind date."

She was absolutely right.

"Tell me what's going on," I said.

He didn't respond right off. He pulled one of his tiny Italian cigars from his inner pocket and lit it with a gold monogrammed lighter. A few of the patrons at the tables across the aisle frowned, but he ignored them. He just blew the smoke at the ceiling fan a few feet beyond our booth and shifted in his seat.

"The thing is," he said in a soft voice, "I don't *know* what the fuck's going on. I don't know who I can trust and who's going behind my back. Just that something *is* going on. A few days ago, I heard from a reliable source that some of my people are considering going over to Paseo's organization. Right after that, Sonny called, said something about some of my merchandise coming up missing."

Merchandise. Papa Joe was talking drugs. Someone had taken a shipment of coke, possibly a shipment earmarked for one of the casinos Papa Joe owned in Biloxi. The load could have been worth a million bucks. It could also have been worth just a few thousand. The point was that it was stolen. You don't steal from a mob boss and live to tell about it.

"Did you find out if it was true?"

"I had a coupla my men check it out. It's true." Papa Joe scanned the room again, appearing more alert, less tired. He was coming back, his anger reviving him. Anger gave him his edge, his superiority. Anger fired up the senses; it also fine-tuned the survival mode.

The blazing coals turned my way. "All this is confidential, *capire*?"

"Why tell me any of this if you don't trust me?"

He nodded. "I'm in a bind, Deacon. Someone lifted eight hundred large from me and I got this sick feeling my most trusted boys are involved."

"Could it be someone as close as Sonny?"

"Christ, I hope not. But I dunno. I don't fucking know, and it's tearing me up."

"I'll bet."

"Can you do this for me? Find out what's going on?"

"I don't know. If it's as complicated as you think--"

"I'll pay you ten grand for this."

Wow. That was much more than I was used to. But I wasn't sure I could handle something this big by myself. Papa Joe's organization employed hundreds of people. If more than one of them had stolen a shipment, my chances of finding out who was involved without getting myself killed were close to nil.

"Not enough?"

"It's not that. . ."

"Tell me your terms." He shrugged. "I can't read your mind."

"It has nothing to do with money."

"What's the problem?"

"I told you what happened to me tonight. It happened even before I knew what was going on. Before you even asked for my help."

Papa Joe sighed deeply. He shook his head. "Somebody flapped his gums."

The hair on the back of my neck bristled. He was holding something back, something important. Whatever it was, it had to do with those two in the Challenger. He did know about this, if not directly. The guilt showed prominently in the way he was avoiding my eyes.

"Who'd you tell about this?"

"About getting you to work for me?"

"Let's start with that."

56

"My business manager. Dan Kelly."

"There ya go. You just found your leak. And it didn't cost you a dime."

"It ain't like that. You can't condemn the man just 'cause he's my business manager. It's too fucking simple. Too obvious. Kelly's handled my affairs for years. He's a shyster, but I still trust him. I didn't want to at first, but over the years he's earned my trust. He's made me--made all of us--a ton of money."

"Who else did you tell about me?"

He didn't speak. He knew something he didn't want to share. Or maybe didn't want to admit he'd told someone something he shouldn't have.

"If Kelly's the only one who knows--"

"It ain't him, Deacon."

"It's got to be someone."

"It ain't Kelly."

"Who else does Kelly work with?"

"He's an attorney. They all got other clients."

"Who?"

Papa Joe shrugged. "How the hell should I know? We're friends, but that don't mean he tells me everything. I'm his biggest client, but he's got others. He's clean, Deacon. *Clean.* He gets two million a year from me, just for managing my assets and doing my taxes. Why the hell would he fuck that up?"

"Maybe someone else offered him three million a year."

He poured more cognac and stubbed out his cigar in the glass ashtray. "You're barking up the wrong tree."

"I know you think he's clean, but word got out that you wanted to hire me. And since you told Kelly about me. . ."

"It ain't him, Deacon."

"What if it is?"

Papa Joe frowned. He forced his eyes shut, trying to keep everything out. He didn't want to think his trusted associate would betray him. It would prove he'd made an error in judgment. A mob boss can't afford the luxury of making such colossal mistakes.

"I have to know why someone wants me dead. Just because you hire me doesn't mean I'm gonna actually find who's doing this to you. I'm not *that* good."

"Whoever wants you dead thinks you are."

He obviously knew more than what he'd told me. "Who else have you told about me?"

He stared at the tabletop. His anger had deserted him again, deflating his ego, his presence. He'd become just another elderly gentleman sitting at a booth, drinking cognac and remembering the good ol' days.

"Well?" I wasn't about to let him stay like that. This involved me, and I needed to know everything.

"That slick move you made with the car bomb two years back."

"Who'd you tell about that?"

He sighed and looked away. Avoiding my eyes again. "It . . . got around."

"I think he helped it along," Mike said suddenly, "without knowing what he was doing."

I was afraid something like that had happened.

"You in, Deacon?" He'd recovered and looked anxious. He no longer avoided my gaze, and the fire in his eyes had returned.

"Like I said before, I don't know if I can handle something this big."

"Haven't you been listening? You're good. That's why someone wants you dead. And that's why I wanna hire you."

"As I said before, they tried getting me hours ago--even before you offered to hire me. This tells me how desperate they are. Once I actually start snooping around and digging up dirt, things are gonna get really bad."

"You want twenty-five? You got it."

A lot of money, but in this case, the actual amount wasn't my prime motivation. You can't spend money when you're dead. "I just don't know if I'm the right guy for this."

"You're a private dick. A good one. This is why they want you dead."

"There are plenty of agencies in town that can do this much more efficiently than I can. Agencies with unlimited money and resources. I can think of two or three who could send out a team that could wrap this up in--"

"Most agencies won't deal with me. My name scares off people."

He was right. Papa Joe was a criminal. Most credible agencies wouldn't even return his call. Being linked to Organized Crime, especially in law enforcement, makes people nervous. This was another reason why I didn't want to be involved. But the old man was in a bind. He trusted me. I'd done him a favor in the past, and he'd done me a couple in turn, mostly by letting me live and continue to run my little business in his city. Favors mean a lot to comrades--especially *paisanos*.

"I want you, Deacon."

My heart sunk. Papa Joe looked pitiful.

But I had to face facts. If I was right about all this, there could be dozens of traitors in the Raguzzo Organization. I just didn't have the means or the resources to handle something this big.

"If only you hadn't told anyone about that car bomb. . ."

"Shit like that gets around. You know how many trained pros coulda found that fucking thing?"

"My biorhythm was on the upswing that day. Otherwise--"

"You're the only one I trust, Deacon."

"You realize I'll probably get killed doing this, don't you?"

"No, you won't," Mike said.

As tactfully as I could, I turned in her direction. She remained invisible--possibly to keep me from being distracted. I managed a slight half-smile.

"If there was anyone else I could trust," Papa Joe said, "I wouldn't ask you. Believe me. You're a smartass. A *stronzone*. But I got to respect someone

60

that can spot a car bomb that don't even look like no car bomb. Besides, you did me that favor last year, with those escort service morons. I respect someone that does me a favor. I come from the old country. Old-fashioned *Italianos* believe in payback. We pay our debts."

"By getting me killed?"

"I won't let anything happen to you," Mike whispered.

"By paying you a ton of money for helping me," he said.

"You know I won't," Mike said.

I turned back to her and gave her another half-smile.

"Whaddya keep looking at?" Papa Joe gazed past me.

"I've got this kink in my neck."

He shrugged. "I got someone who can fix shit like that."

"I'll bet he does kneecaps, too."

"Such a smartass." He shook his head and poured more cognac. "Your poor momma."

"She knows all about me. She loves me anyway."

He grunted. "She's got to. She's your momma."

"That's beside the point."

"Well?" Papa Joe put down the bottle heavily. He'd grown impatient and wanted to end this. He had things to do, people to manage.

"What was that price again?"

"You forget already?"

"I just want to hear it again."

"Twenty-five large."

That amount could pay the rent for my apartment as well as my office for several months. It could even put groceries in the fridge and a couple of bottles of whiskey in my cupboard.

"I'll have it deposited into your bank account on Monday morning."

"What happens if I don't make it through the weekend? My ex-wife'll be very upset if she has to pay for my funeral."

Papa Joe reached into his pocket, removed a thick wad of hundred-dollar-bills, peeled off ten and dropped them on the table. "There's a grand. Just to get you through the next two days."

"Funerals are expensive. I'm sure Phil will want a viewing, and one of those big stones that tell you when--"

"*Dammit*, Deacon. *I'll* pay for your funeral!" He slammed his palm on the table. Several people at other tables jumped, jerking their faces in our direction. Papa Joe didn't notice. He simply peeled off another thousand and added it to the pile. "*There*, dammit. Two grand, just to get you through the weekend. You got that, plus my personal pledge as a businessman and respected member of the Catholic Church that everything will be taken care of if anything happens to you. Sound better?"

"I guess . . ." I didn't want to get him any more riled than he already was.

"You gonna take this or what?" His eyes turned back into burning coals. The anger and superiority also returned.

"Sure. Bring it on."

Papa Joe stared at me. He wanted to smile, but he wasn't the sort of man who smiles very much. Instead, he nodded and patted my right thigh.

I would have preferred a smile. But when a mob boss pats your thigh, the worst thing you can do is tell him to keep his hands to himself.

Chapter Five

After my talk with Papa Joe, I was skeptical about getting back into the limo.

The chauffeur was the same guy who'd brought me to the restaurant, but I forced myself to consider the facts. This man had already delivered me safely to Papa Joe. That alone should be enough to help soothe my fears, but it didn't. The driver might have done the deed so he wouldn't draw attention to himself. If I'd been killed on the way to Dante's, Papa Joe would know right off who was responsible.

Since I'd talked with Papa Joe, I'd become fair game. I'd been hired by Papa Joe to find out what was going on. And since everyone in the organization had apparently been told how good a snoop I was, I'd become a major threat.

I'd left my gun in my apartment. Needless to say, it didn't make me feel any better.

"You're nervous," Mike said, appearing beside me in the back seat. She'd turned visible again, and looked fetching in her red tee shirt and jeans.

I nodded.

"The driver bumming you out?"

I caught him glancing at me in his rearview.

"You can talk, you know," Mike said. "That piece of glass over the seat looks pretty thick. I didn't see him switch on any microphones, so he can't possibly hear us."

"It's not his hearing I'm worried about," I whispered, rubbing my nose to hide my lips from view.

"What are you worried about?"

"He'll see me talking." I continued rubbing my nose.

"He might think you're just talking to yourself."

"I shouldn't be doing that."

"You're worried about what a chauffeur thinks of you?"

I didn't want it getting around that I talked to myself. If Papa Joe found out, he'd think I was crazy. Like most Italians, he was probably superstitious and wouldn't want to deal with someone having mental issues.

I reached up and rubbed my eye. "I don't want anyone thinking I might be crazy."

"You are sometimes, you know."

"It helps in this business. But thanks a lump for the evaluation."

"I'm kidding. But I just don't think this guy is someone to worry about."

"Hope you're right."

He turned off Colonial and went south on Maguire.

So far, so good. He was taking the same route he'd used on the way to Dante's. If he got onto Crystal Lake Road and took it straight to Curry Ford, I'd start breathing again.

Ten minutes later, the limo pulled into my complex and stopped in front of my apartment building. I glanced at my watch. Just a few minutes before midnight.

The chauffeur made a move to get out.

"It's all right, I can get it." I opened my door.

He got out and quickly pulled open my door. "My job, sir."

"Thanks." I felt ridiculous, having a guy open a car door for me.

"Good evening, sir." He closed the door, got in behind the wheel and drove off.

I pulled my keys out of my pants pocket. Before crossing the street, I scanned the lot. No movement or suspicious vehicles. Aside from the usual nighttime traffic zipping up and down Conway and a couple of cicadas squawking loudly in the bushes, everything was quiet.

Just as I turned to approach the curb, Mike appeared, drifting down the short grassy slope toward me. Her face, somewhat blurry, looked troubled. "Those two guys we saw earlier," she said, stopping just a couple of feet from me. "They're in your apartment."

***

My first impulse was to run down the street and slip between the buildings.

I could hide behind a palmetto and wait for them to get tired of all this and just drive away.

Or *I* could drive away. The TransAm sat quietly in its space, less than fifty feet away. I could just mosey on over, get inside and take off down the street--

"They're watching through the peephole." Mike saw me glance at the TransAm. "If they think you're suspicious, they'll come right out and shoot you. They both have their guns out. They were screwing on silencers when I left. They look really angry."

Of course they were angry; I'd given them the slip. They wouldn't let me get away this time.

"Any suggestions?" I whispered.

"How often does that guard makes his rounds?"

The guard stationed in the tiny building near the Conway entrance was tall, gangly and well over seventy. He showed up at ten each night and sat on the hard stool inside the sixteen-square-foot shelter until six in the morning. He was supposed to make his rounds every hour, but I'd seen him make only two or three quick trips around the complex each night. He spent most of his time on the padded stool, napping, smoking his pipe or working crossword puzzles beneath the single overhead bulb.

"He usually comes around at midnight, two, and four o'clock."

"What time is it?"

"Almost midnight." I snatched another peek at my watch and kept my back turned so my would-be killers wouldn't see me talking.

"Give me a minute. I'll see what he's doing."

"He's probably taking a nap."

"I'll make sure he does his midnight rounds."

"How?"

"Don't ask questions. I'll be right back."

"What'll I do while you're waking the guard?"

"Act like you just got a call. Pull out your cell and dial nine-one-one. Get the cops here as fast as you can."

"What about the guard? I don't want him getting in the way."

"He'll be good cover and a possible eyewitness."

"What if they kill him, too?"

"Then you'll both be dead, and we won't have to worry any more, silly." Then she disappeared.

I took two steps toward the complex, stopped suddenly and fished for my cell. I pulled it out and flicked it open. For the benefit of the two watching through my peephole, I tried reading the display, then moved over to the streetlamp to see it better. I thumbed 911 and brought it up to my cheek.

"Emergency operator," the female voice came on.

"This is Ralph Deacon. Two men just broke into my apartment. They're in there right now, and they both have guns."

"What is your address, sir?"

I gave it to her.

"Where are you now?"

"Outside my apartment."

"How do you know about the men?"

"I, uh, was warned by a neighbor when I got out of my car. She has a good view of the place and saw guns in their hands. I'm a private detective and have connections with OPD."

"Help is on the way."

"Thanks."

"Please stay on the line, sir."

"No problem." I walked around with the phone in my ear, nodding occasionally. The cops seldom used their sirens at this time of night. In a neighborhood where so many elderly people lived, using a siren could be deadly. I hoped they'd get here before the two in my apartment grew impatient.

Footsteps behind me.

I turned. The guard, shuffling in his usual slow gait, approached. "You're out late tonight," he said, coughing wetly.

"Really? I hadn't noticed." I felt much safer in the presence of such an observant security guard.

"Talkin' to someone?" He jabbed an arthritic finger at my cell.

The old boy really was on the ball.

"An old friend."

"How come you're not talkin' to 'im, then?"

"He's telling me a story. I never interrupt him when he's telling me a story. It makes him go back to the beginning and start all over."

The guard grunted. "Nice night." He glanced up at the starry sky.

"Yeah. Real nice."

He shook his head. "Those damn cicadas, they never shuddup."

"They're probably arguing about who should let out the cat."

The guard watched me for a few moments. He was probably trying to figure out if I was serious. He finally shrugged and reached inside his jacket pocket for his curved briar pipe. He filled it with

69

tobacco, used his thumb to stuff the bowl and lit up. The thick, gray smoke billowed heavily in my direction. I waved it away. He didn't notice as he puffed away.

"Lotta traffic tonight." He blew a thick plume toward the lake behind the buildings on our right.

"Just like all other nights."

"Seems heavier than usual."

I hated small talk. A lot of stupidity and nonsense comes out of a person's mouth when he's bored and doesn't have anything intelligent to say. Men are more awkward with small talk than women and always revert to mock insults and other silliness when they have nothing to say and don't want to be accused of being unfriendly.

"Could be more tourists than usual comin' down." He hawked out a jolt of tobacco juice and missed my shoe by a couple of inches. I stepped back and hoped the cruisers would get here. He was getting on my nerves, and I didn't want to get arrested for wiping my shoe on an elderly security guard's ass.

"That's probably it. Tourists."

"Yep. Tourists." He sucked down more tobacco smoke, pushing out a slim plume at me. I ducked out of the way, but some of it landed in my hair, clinging to it like cobwebs.

Thankfully, the flashing blue lights penetrated the darkness as the cruisers crept up to us. One of them used the straight stretch while the other turned left and snuck up through the back way. Both vehicles stopped about ten feet from where the guard and I stood.

"Wh-What's all this?" The old man practically dropped his pipe.

"Just stand back and let them work," I said.

"Sir?" The operator was trying to get my attention. "Has help arrived?"

"Yes. Thank you."

One of the cops--Sillman, according to his name tag--recognized me. He hurried right over, his gun drawn, while his partner got out from behind the wheel and snuck up the short grassy slope to my front door. Sillman put an index finger to his mouth and waved us back. I grabbed the old man's bony elbow and pulled him behind the first cruiser. He coughed wetly again, spitting out more tobacco juice and smearing the cruiser's fender and front tire.

The other two officers got out quickly. Leaving both doors open, they snuck onto the lawn on the other side of the building. One of them stopped a few feet from my dining room window, his gun pointed out, while his partner circled around to the rear. I expected the second guy to come back around and stop in front of my bedroom window on the south side of the building.

Sillman's partner stopped a few feet from the stoop, his gun held in both hands, pointed straight at the door. He yelled, "Police! Come out with your hands up!"

No response.

"This is the police! Both of you drop your weapons and come out with your hands up!"

Still nothing.

A few moments of dead silence.

Then: Doc Severinsen's Command Performance of "*When the Saints Come Marching In*" blasted from my apartment.

The door jerked open. The two men hurried out, arms raised high as they dropped to their knees.

Sillman and his partner rushed over and cuffed them in the grass.

***

My pulse raced long after the police had taken my statement.

I'd escaped death twice in one evening. The more I thought about it, the more it scared me. What frightened me most was that it happened out of the blue, after a relaxing evening at a restaurant. And the fact that the two hitters waited for me later on, in my apartment, made me wonder if my ex-wife Phil had been right about my career choice.

Even so, the evening wasn't a total loss.

Twenty-five thousand smackeroos. A lot of jack--especially for a job that might only take a few days. It was going to be dangerous--possibly tougher than anything I'd ever done. I'd be stupid to think otherwise. You don't go snooping around a mob boss's back yard and expect to make friends.

Such details shouldn't bother me at all. I didn't have many friends to begin with. People bugged me. They acted stupid and talked stupid, and if you found fault with them, they got huffy and considered you antisocial. I knew a lot of people and had a lot of acquaintances, but with the

72

exception of Mike and Phil, I couldn't think of anyone I actually wanted to spend time with.

Besides, I didn't have time for friends. I spent my days in my Orange Avenue office, waiting for something to happen, or sniffing around Orlando on a case. I sometimes got roughed up. On other occasions, knocked out. I didn't like it, but it came with the territory.

Snooping around for Papa Joe shouldn't be any different.

Mike had told me not to worry. Under normal circumstances, I'd consider her advice meaningless and stupid. But the circumstances weren't normal. Mike was dead. More importantly, she'd saved my life twice in one night.

Right now she was in the dining room, watching me as I had another shot of whiskey to settle my nerves. As I grew more relaxed, my thoughts stopped looping. A few urgent questions shot right to the surface.

"What the hell did you do to those two?" I couldn't stop wondering what had happened in here while I was outside, dodging tobacco juice. "I've never seen two more frightened hit men in my life."

She smiled. "Just a few tricks to keep them busy until the police came."

"What kind of tricks?"

"They were about to open the door and shoot you right there in the street, so I went down the hall to distract them. I drifted into your bedroom and let them hear me cough." She laughed. "They stormed down the hall and stood in the doorway, pointing their guns and flashlights at me. It was hilarious, but it didn't keep them away from the front door for very long. They figured they were just jumpy, so they went back to the peephole. I went into the bathroom and cleared my throat, and in just a few seconds, they were peeking into the room with their guns and flashlights again."

"By this time, the cops were probably already on their way."

"I decided these two needed a little shove, so I summoned all my power and flicked the CD player on full power as soon as they went back to the front door. This was right after they heard the cop ordering them outside."

"Sometimes you're a true genius." I hoisted my glass.

"I thought the music thing was a nice touch."

"You thought right." I finished my drink and poured another inch into my glass.

"What happens now?"

"I've got to go into the station tomorrow morning and explain all this to my friend Neil."

"Explain all what?"

"They're gonna take this seriously, believe me. Two professional hitters in the South Conway area? This place is crawling with the geriatric crowd. If this had turned into a gunfight, every hospital in the area would've had to dispatch every ambulance they own to come out here and pick up the heart attack victims."

"You won't tell your friend my part in this, will you?"

"You're kidding, right?"

"Of course I'm kidding."

"That would be stupid, even for me."

"It would also annoy me. I get upset when I'm annoyed."

"You're always saving my life. Why would I purposely do something to annoy you? I'm not *that* dumb."

"You've got a good point."

"You could've argued, you know."

"About what?"

"My being dumb."

"I don't want you to get a swelled head."

"Can't happen. Too many people standing in line, waiting to take a poke at it."

"So then . . . do you want me to come with you tomorrow?"

"Do you want to?"

"Why wouldn't I?"

"You might have other plans."

"Like what?"

I shrugged. "Breakfast with Flo and her friends? Another gab session with that dead babe you met at Charley's? For all I know, you might want to do a haunting in one of the old churches downtown."

"That's silly. Everyone knows it's stupid to try to haunt a place in the morning."

"Why?"

"People aren't nearly as scared in the mornings."

"I never thought of that."

"On a serious note, of course I'll come . . . if you want me there with you."

"Why am I sensing hesitation?"

"I don't want to get you in any more trouble."

"How could you possibly do that?"

"I might say something at the wrong time. I've done that before, you know."

"Have I ever complained?"

"Well . . . you did say a few choice things when I showed up at your mom's. . ."

"We were dealing with my relatives. Relatives tend to mess up the balance in the universe. At least mine do."

"I understand. But I did like your mom. She's pretty."

"I'll pass along your compliment."

Exhaustion signaled, the evening catching up, and my legs suddenly weighed a ton. "I've got to get to bed. If I don't show up at the station by nine, Neil will probably be calling me."

"Good night, then." She began fading.

I checked the front door and the sliding glass door in the dining room, then the living room and bedroom windows. Satisfied, I turned off the lights and staggered down the hall.

I was fast asleep in minutes.

Chapter Six - Saturday

Neil Haversack appeared more surly than usual when I went into his office at OPD Headquarters a little after nine.

Mike hadn't shown up yet, so I was on my own. Neil's chubby cheeks displayed more reddish-blond stubble than normal. His tiny blue eyes were glazed and puffy. He also looked like he'd dressed in a hurry. His collar was lopsided, his tie twisted. He'd either had an argument with his wife or his ulcers were giving him trouble.

"Heard about your rough night." He backed up from the coffee station and set a steaming cup of thick black battery acid on the desk near my elbow. He lowered his butt into the chair, opened the top drawer and grabbed a fistful of sugar packets and creamers, dumping them on the green blotter.

The heat from the cup singed the hair in my nostrils, forcing me to keep away from the table. I didn't want to spill the coffee on Neil's desk and melt the blotter, and I surely didn't want to piss him off by accidentally dropping the cup in the trashcan. After Papa Joe's cognac the night before, I wanted to baby my stomach for a little while.

"I've had better. But it didn't disturb my sleep too much."

"Really?" Neil sounded skeptical.

"I chose a rough profession. If I let every little thing bug me--"

"Two contract killers showed up in your apartment."

"That more or less sums it up."

"And you'd call that a *little* thing?"

"Well, when you put it *that* way. . ."

Neil dumped three sugars and two creamers into his cup and stirred it with a red plastic stirrer. It stayed black, but at least it didn't melt the stirrer. "How else can I put it?"

"It got resolved very quickly. No one was hurt."

His eyes stayed on me, blinking as they usually did whenever his radar was switched on. "I'd say there's a little more to it than that, wouldn't you?"

This wasn't going to be easy. Things seldom were with Neil.

"That's what happened."

His eyes stopped blinking and grew, staying on me. He'd just picked up something, sensed something wrong. "To be perfectly blunt, this reeks."

I had to sound casual. Otherwise, he'd pick up something else. Neil was good with vocal inflections. He might have once been a dog in a former life.

"What reeks about it?"

He had a small sip of coffee, grimaced and put the cup back down. "Just about everything."

"Please explain. I'm somewhat confused."

"For one thing, both Dillman and his partner Sanchez said they'd never had an easier collar, and they've got more than thirty years of collars between them."

"What does that have to do with anything?"

"We're talking contract killers, Deacon. Professional wet boys. Hitters. Sociopaths that get paid top dollar for killing people. They're a dangerous breed. They don't get arrested-- especially in the middle of a job. It's, well, embarrassing. And it doesn't do their reputations any good."

Neil was already putting things together. That's what was so aggravating about him. You had to be careful about telling him anything. I felt sorry for his wife.

"A couple of things made this happen the way it did," I said.

"I had a feeling you were about to tell me something like that." He sat back and rested the back of his head in his large hands. "Hopefully, this'll sound more convincing as I hear the facts from your end. Dillman's report was pretty straightforward, but I have this strange feeling some minor details were missing."

"What was lacking in the police report?"

He brought his arms back down and sat forward. "They said you called in a nine-one-one about two armed men in your apartment."

"That's pretty accurate."

Neil's crooked collar was bugging me. I straightened my own and hoped he'd take the hint and follow suit.

Instead, he had another sip of the boiling battery acid. He put down the cup. His stomach groaned. I felt sorry for it.

"You really expect me to believe this went down that easy?" he asked.

"What sounds wrong about it?"

"As I said before, two contract killers aren't caught that easy. They wouldn't've been caught together, for one thing. If they'd wanted you bad enough and were being paid enough, they would've split up. One in your apartment and the other outside, hiding somewhere convenient."

"Maybe they weren't contract killers at all."

Neil rubbed his eyes and squinted, looking at me in that unsettling way that suggested he was ready to go at this another way. "No, just two gun nuts who decided to spend their Friday night in your apartment, waiting for the police to show up."

"What I meant was, maybe they were two rookies on their first job."

"See their guns?"

"The cops grabbed them before I had a chance to look them over."

"Makarovs, both of them."

Bummer. Cheap, easy to buy, and even easier to dump. A popular choice with professional hitters. This was getting more and more difficult to explain. But I couldn't possibly tell Neil what really happened.

"So?" I figured I'd let him take this where he wanted to go with it.

"Disposable pieces. Wet boys use them almost exclusively for close work. Serials were filed down. Butts were taped. And the silencers were the kind anyone can buy online for a hundred bucks."

I decided to stay vague and clueless. Otherwise, Neil would be even more suspicious. I couldn't handle that. Neil turned into a major pain in the ass when he suspected something screwy.

"What are you getting at?"

"These two were pros. You knew they were pros, so stop trying to bullshit me."

"How would I know they were pros?"

"We both know what they are. Oh . . . and while we're on the subject, something else about this fiasco needs to be explained to me. Why the hell would two hitters turn on big band music before surrendering to the police?"

Oh boy . . . I'd forgotten about that. I should've had a workable lie ready, should've figured Dillman and the other cops would include it in their reports.

"Well?"

"They, uh, didn't turn it on, Neil. I did."

"From the parking lot?"

"I've got this friend who dabbles in electronics. I asked him to rig me a remote device that'll flick on my lights before I go inside. I didn't know it would come in handy at such a convenient time."

"This was music--not the lights."

"I have the lights and the CD player on the same switch. I must've had the CD ready to go when--"

81

"You thought you'd just turn the lights on and shake them up a little?"

My grin was weak. "Something like that."

"You know I can check this out, right?"

"It's the truth."

Neil gave me his look again, letting me know he didn't buy it. If it didn't sound right, it wasn't true, and should be checked out. I just hoped he'd let it go. I didn't know if I could find an electronics guy on such short notice.

"It really is," I said, trying to look innocent.

His gaze did not waver. "I've known you for years. I can tell you're hiding something."

"Me? Hiding something?"

"Sounds incredible, doesn't it?"

I wished Mike would show up. I was running out of clever explanations, and my devil-may-care attitude was wearing thin. Besides, Neil was running out of patience. I decided to steer him down another path.

"Have they been questioned yet?"

"They spent the night in our interview rooms with four of our best detectives. The perps were separated, of course, and we took our time letting them make their calls."

Hopefully they'd found out who those two were working for. "So you had plenty of time to find out a few things, then."

"They didn't say a word. That's another reason why I know they're pros. Pros don't scare. Not at all. You can't scare them, intimidate them, or bribe them. We could've brought in a batch of strippers from one of the clubs on the Trail and those two wouldn't've raised a brow."

"Maybe they're gay."

His eyes stayed on me. "Not the point and you know it."

I sighed. This was not going well at all.

"Deacon, who the hell are you working for?"

I tried extra hard not to look like someone with an angry wasp wandering around in my undershorts. "What . . . makes you think I'm working for anyone?"

"Like I said before, I know you. You never get into trouble unless you're working for someone."

"I didn't realize I was so predictable."

"I know you're working for someone."

"Then you also know I can't tell you who my employer is."

"You're gonna pull that confidential crap on me now?"

"I have to. Otherwise, I won't get any more clients."

If Neil knew I was working for Papa Joe, he'd have my ass on a spit. Working for a mob boss was a no-no with the cops. It made them think you were on the underworld's payroll and couldn't be trusted. Cops tended to be horrible snobs about some things.

"This is serious, Deacon. You came close tonight."

"I come close a lot."

"Two contract killers? In your apartment? How the hell did you sniff them out in the first place?"

"Tell them what you told the operator last night." Mike appeared next to me in a white sleeveless V-neck blouse and black-and-gold checkered skirt. Her hair was freshly brushed. I didn't know if ghosts did things like that, or just concentrated on polishing up their image. But whatever she'd done sure made her look spectacular.

I sighed in relief.

"What's so funny?" Neil asked.

I blinked. "Funny?"

"You've got that stupid grin on your face."

"Which one? I have several I carry around with me."

"The one you always flash right before you tell me something totally convincing, logical and unbelievable. It's either that, or you just let loose with a foul one. I don't smell anything, so . . ."

"I think I get it."

"Good. Now tell me how you knew two contract killers were in your apartment."

I decided to follow Mike's advice. It was the only thing I could say that wouldn't get me in further trouble. But I had to be subtle and mildly evasive about it. Otherwise, I'd have to produce someone to verify what I was about to say. I didn't want any of my neighbors involved.

It was bad enough this happened in the first place. The cops had acted efficiently and quietly enough, but even so, many of my neighbors had heard the commotion or seen the blinking lights and wandered outside. And when a bunch of people congregated together to watch a crime scene, they grew instantly chatty.

"One of my neighbors saved my life," I finally said.

Neil squinted, watching me closely. He was trying to decide if that was the truth. It took only a moment before he shook his head, indicating his skepticism. *No go, Deacon. Try again. Let's work this my way now so I can get to the actual truth.* "One of your neighbors told you two contract killers were in your apartment, waiting for you?"

"Actually, a relative one of my neighbors asked me if I was having a party."

"What are you doing?" Mike asked.

I gave her a quick glare.

"What's the glare for?" Neil asked.

"Reflux. That coffee's strong."

"You haven't even tried it."

"Sniffing it was enough to send my stomach into hysterical spasms."

"Whatever. But do go on." He tapped his watch. "I have other things to do this morning."

"I was getting out of my car and she was walking across the street--"

"Who?"

"Hazel."

"She's a neighbor?"

"She comes over from time to time to visit her ailing grandmother. Nice lady, this woman."

"Who? Hazel? Or her mother?"

"Both, actually. Hazel's about ten years older than me, and really keeps in shape. She's always on that tennis court, and I've even seen her in the pool, doing laps--"

"Get on with this." Neil was not amused.

"Your friend sure is nasty," Mike said.

"Yeah," I told her.

"Yeah what?" Neil asked, glaring.

"Yeah, I'll get on with this."

"Goody." Neil's glare remained. "We're both getting older by the second."

"Anyway, she stopped and asked me about the two men in my apartment."

"And?"

"She said she saw them taking something out of their jacket pockets as they were going inside."

"And of course you automatically assumed these were two contract killers with guns and silencers. . ."

"I assumed something was going on."

"How?"

"Wouldn't you expect trouble if you didn't invite anyone to your place and found out two men had let themselves in anyway?"

"Good point."

"Besides, I've never given my key to anyone."

"You weren't . . . expecting something like this, by any chance, were ya?"

"I guess you could say I was in a suspicious frame of mind, yes."

"And why's that?"

"My new client, well, he's got someone after him."

"I take it this new client isn't exactly a man of the cloth."

"He never did tell me his religion."

"You know what I mean, dammit."

"He told me someone's after him, and he wants me to find out who it is."

"Well, I'm sure you have a pretty good idea who it is now, don'tcha?"

"Not really."

"Those two hitters didn't give you some sort of clue that your new client might not be an upstanding member of society?"

"Neil, sometimes you can be such a snob. . ."

"Can it, Deacon. I'm trying to find out what's going on. This isn't something to take lightly, you know."

"Sounds like you're worried about me."

"I'm being practical. If someone takes you out, I'm gonna have to spend countless man-hours looking for your killers."

"I knew you had a soft spot."

"Yeah, and it happens to be located between my ears. I'm also chickenshit when it comes to women--especially when they're on a rampage."

"What are you getting at now?"

"Your ex-wife is what I'm getting at. You know she'll be on my case like ants on a dead mouse if something happens to you and she finds out I knew something about it."

"Maybe I'd better not leave her my gun collection in my will as I'd planned, then . . ."

"I'm serious, Deacon. If this new client is into heavy stuff, you need to bail."

"I'm being paid a lot of--"

"I don't give a rat's ass how much you're being paid. If you're dodging contract killers, your client is not worth working for."

"Now what kind of detective would I be if I turned down a high-paying job just because I didn't approve of my client's line of work?"

"A live one."

"I'm okay, Neil."

"What do you mean, okay?"

"I've got someone looking out for me."

"You've told me that before."

"It's true. The tips I've been getting have helped me squeeze out of some tight spots many times in the last couple of years."

"I've noticed. I also know that this weird streak of good luck is liable to end one of these days."

"Like I said, I've got some good inside tips."

"This doesn't mean you're immune to a bullet."

"I stand a much better chance of dodging one if I know exactly where it's coming from and when."

The phone rang. He picked it up, swiveled his chair around and spoke softly into it.

"He's skeptical," Mike said.

"I know," I whispered.

Neil swiveled back around and put the phone back down. "I guess we're done with those two hitters--whoever they were."

"Were?"

"They're out."

"Out?"

"Their high-priced attorney sprung them."

I sat bolt upright--as if the imaginary wasp in my undershorts had found a sensitive spot. "You mean . . . they're actually . . . out? Free? Wandering around again?"

Neil had some coffee. "I'm *so* glad you've been paying attention."

"But . . . they broke in. What about that?"

"I was just told there were no signs of forced entry."

"They picked the lock, then."

"Something like that."

"What about their guns? They also had silencers. Silencers are illegal, last I checked."

"That's another fly in the ointment. The guns were found lying on your couch."

Smart. For two guys who couldn't seem to get me, they knew exactly what they were doing. "You know those guns aren't mine, Neil . . ."

"Yeah. I do."

"Then surely you must know--"

"No serial numbers. No prints. Their attorney knows all the tricks. He'll whittle this one down to third degree trespassing, which comes with three months in prison, tops, a five-hundred-dollar fine, or both. You know in this case, it'll be neither because it won't even come to trial. Even if it does, you know how we feel about these cases."

"Nuisance offenses."

"Exactly. And you know we won't spend any time at all to prosecute a nuisance offense."

I was nailed, plain and simple. They didn't get me, but they were out again. Out again and wandering around, working up a good mad for what I did to them twice in one night.

My pulse settled down and my brain started working again. "Do you happen to know the name of the attorney who sprung them?"

"Not offhand. Is it important?"

Neil could be a real butthole at times.

"You know it is."

"I'll call you the instant I find out."

If it turned out to be Kelly, my job was done. All I had to do then was tell Papa Joe and tell him.

"Does that meet with your approval?" Neil's vibes were heavy and easy to read. He'd finished with my story and wanted me to leave so he could get back to work.

"Sure does. We're good to go."

"We're pleased." He scribbled something illegible on his calendar. "I'll make sure I get that to you."

"So where does this leave me?"

Neil snorted. "You're obviously a prime target for a couple of wet boys. I may be wrong, but I'd hazard a guess and say they won't make any mistakes when they come after you the next time."

"You don't exactly sound sympathetic, you know."

"There's a really good reason for that."

"I know. You're about to get on me for accepting a high-paying job from a shady client."

"There ya go."

"As I already said, I can't turn down a job just because I might not approve of my client's profession."

"Deacon, we've just been through all this. I already told you how stupid you were for that, and you told me in your own smartassed way why you couldn't turn the job down. I'd say we're both done here."

"And what about the two hitters that just walked out of the building?"

Neil shrugged, picked up his coffee and took another careful sip. "I'd tell you to be careful, but I'm sure you already know."

"Thanks for the heads-up." I found it irritating that he was more interested in my leaving than about the two hitters after me.

"You're welcome."

"Before I leave, I've got to tell you something that's been bugging me since I came in."

"Will this give me some idea who you're working for so we can at least keep an eye out for your pitiful ass?"

"Not exactly. . ."

"What is it, then?"

"Your collar's crooked. So is your tie. Fix it. You look like a schmuck."

Chapter Seven

The parking garage next to OPD was half-empty--which was normal for a Saturday morning.

No one walking about or looking suspicious, and the TransAm appeared to be undisturbed. As a precaution, I dropped to my knees and peered underneath to see if there were any wires dangling beneath the body, as in the case with the car bomb Mike had warned me about, two years earlier.

"It's safe," she said, drifting closer.

Relieved, I got behind the wheel and closed the door. Mike appeared beside me. I pulled the .380 out of the console and set it on the lid of the console. I didn't even care if it could be seen during a traffic stop. I wanted to be able to grab it in a hurry.

Before pulling out, I scanned the vehicles parked beside me and across the aisle. The concrete ceiling engulfed the open area in a shadowy eeriness, making everything gray and frighteningly ominous.

Keeping my imagination in check, I opened the window and listened for the usual threats--sudden footsteps, the clicking of a knife, or the cocking of a hammer. I heard only traffic sounds on Hughey Avenue, a distant car horn, and a car door slamming shut on another level.

I had to close this case quickly. Regardless of how much money Papa Joe was paying me, I didn't want to live like this. If I had to spend the rest of my life jumping at shadows and noises, I'd be ready for the nuthouse very soon.

I pulled out and eased down the ramp.

"Your friend isn't very nice," Mike said.

"He's got his good points."

"He acts like he doesn't care if you're killed."

"He has to sound tough. He *is* a cop, after all. The Station's a huge drum sloshing with testosterone."

"He's so mean . . . and sarcastic. . ."

"He was just getting back at me."

"For what?"

"For not telling him about my new client."

"So he really does care if you're killed?"

"I'm sure he'll come to my funeral and curse me silly for turning myself into a corpse."

"How can they let two killers go? They broke into your place."

"You heard what Neil said."

"I heard, all right, but to me, all this sounds pretty incriminating."

"Not when the two hitters left their hardware on my couch and made sure their prints were wiped clean. Criminals are a lot smarter nowadays."

"They're killers. And they committed a crime. I think this stinks."

"Welcome to the modern world of high-priced attorneys for the rich and criminally educated." I pulled out onto Hughey and stayed with the flow, glancing at the rearview and side mirrors, as well as the vehicles in front of us.

"They could be anywhere, you know," Mike said.

"I'm sure they'll lay low for a while. It would probably be best for them to leave the country--if they're still alive, that is."

"You think they might be dead?"

"It's possible."

"You mean whoever's doing this has hit guys to go after the other hit guys?"

"You got it."

"It almost sounds like they're all sitting around, playing cards, and when the phone rings, they get up from the table, walk outside, get in their cars and hunt someone down."

"I don't know if they actually sit around and play cards. . ."

"Or like a group of fire fighters. They might even slide down a pole. . ."

"Don't be silly."

"I tend to get that way when things don't make sense. I've only been dead a few years, but people seem much meaner than they used to be. Why do you think those two hit guys might be dead?"

"Contracts are taken very seriously by everyone--especially the big shots ordering the hits. A contract is expensive, for one thing. And if it isn't handled properly, it's sure to get the cops sniffing around. When the cops enter the picture, the mob guys can be arrested, questioned, and detained. The bad guys can lose a bunch of business at the very least, and if one of the bosses is arrested, the organization suffers. When a hitter messes up, he won't get another chance. If he's given one, he'd better deliver. These two messed up twice. That's the kiss of death."

"Then we shouldn't be worried about them anymore?"

"We should be more worried about someone else taking their place."

***

Mike and I got back to my apartment at around eleven.

While Mike did another quick check of the premises, I scanned the parking lot. I heard some activity in the pool and saw four people--two men and two women, all around forty--going at it on the tennis court. A couple of unfamiliar cars sat in spaces across the aisle. A silver SUV, a light-blue Porsche, and an older model black Mercedes. The plates were local and easy to read; none were smudged with mud.

Mike drifted inside my apartment and came right back out, nodding that everything was okay. I crossed the street, opened the apartment door and slipped inside.

I went into the kitchen, opened a cabinet drawer, grabbed the Orlando Phone Directory, thumped it on the counter and flipped it open. Then I picked up the magnifying glass I kept in the same drawer to help me read the endless columns of microscopic names. "I've got to check out Dan Kelly."

"Who?"

"Papa Joe's attorney."

"You actually think he might be the one responsible for all this?"

"I have no idea."

"But your mob boss friend said--"

"I don't care what he said. And he's not my friend, he's my employer. We're talking about two pros who came after me twice last night. Now they're out of jail and probably planning to come at me again. Papa Joe trusts Kelly, but that doesn't mean I have to. The man's an *attorney*, for God's sake."

"That doesn't mean he's guilty of anything, does it? And it certainly doesn't mean he has anything to do with these two hitters."

"Have you ever known an attorney who was innocent of anything?"

"I never knew many attorneys when I was alive. . ."

"Well, I've known several, and believe me, they haven't changed much since you died."

**

Kelly kept two offices—one in downtown Orlando, the other on Semoran Boulevard, in a small strip mall in the Casselberry area.

Kelly's home address was listed on Red Bug Road, which explained his need for an office closer to his home. Traffic on Red Bug and Semoran would be too hectic for a busy attorney to cope with. Alternating his time between offices would be the sensible way to go.

Kelly's Casselberry office sat in the center of the building, sandwiched between a used DVD store and an Italian restaurant.

It did my heart good to see a successful attorney operating in the same atmosphere as my own modest business. I decided not to dwell too much on the glittering white Lexus sitting out front, or the man's purported seven-figure paycheck. He'd probably have fine furniture in both offices and one of those fancy coffeemakers that fixes specialty coffee by the cup. I imagined a dressing room in there, as well. Maybe even a closet with a few tailored suits.

There were more important things in life than money. Kelly couldn't possibly boast a more exciting lifestyle than mine.

At a few minutes after twelve, I parked beside the Lexus and killed the ignition. The sign on his darkly tinted glass door listed his hours. Saturdays were from eleven to one. I'd figured he was here. The Lexus sitting directly in front of his office door had to be his.

I tried ignoring the expensive ride but caught myself staring at it anyway. That model went for sixty, maybe seventy K, with one of those special a/c systems where each passenger could control his own temperature. Cruise control probably went on when the driver thought about it, and the seats undoubtedly had lumbar support and even a massage option.

Enough. The man earned two million a year from Papa Joe just for doing his books and fudging his taxes. He should be able to afford a fleet of expensive rides. Not a bad gig, actually. I should be jealous. And I was. But now was not the time to fixate on that.

"Why aren't we getting out?" Mike asked.

"I'm thinking." I should ask her to go in first and sniff around. Since he wouldn't be able to see her, she could watch what he was doing, maybe even listen in on a phone call. When she learned something, she could come back out and--

"Are you still thinking?"

I sighed. "It's hard to concentrate when someone keeps talking to you."

"Sorry. . ."

"Since you mentioned it, I might have sort of a plan worked out. It involves you."

"Great! What am I going to do?"

"I'd like you to drift inside and take a look at things."

"Like that time I went into that fake travel agency and spied on that snotty receptionist who thought you were old and not funny at all?"

I hated it when she remembered stuff like that. Women always remembered things you wanted them to forget. "Thanks so much for reminding me."

"She only thought you were old because she was really young. And silly. And stupid. Does that help?"

I hated it even worse when a woman brought up something painful and immediately tried softening the blow. "Listen. And pay attention. This time, we're dealing with an attorney, so we're not gonna find anything incriminating. Nothing obvious, anyway."

"What exactly do you want me to do?"

"Just go on in and do what you do. If he's on the phone, listen in and try to find out who he's talking to. Zoom in so you can get close enough to hear the other voice."

"And if he's not talking to anyone?"

"See if he's got something written on his desk calendar."

"Like what?"

"Anything that mentions the Police Station."

"That's right. We have to know if he's the one who bailed those two out of jail."

"If we find out he's the guilty one, I can tell Papa Joe and my job will be finished."

"But what if I can't find anything?"

"Come back out and tell me. Then I'll go in and help the process along."

"You mean you're gonna get him all upset."

"You know me pretty well, don't you?"

"Yep. I sure do." Then she disappeared.

***

Two minutes later, she reappeared beside me in the seat. "He's really got everything done up nicely in there," she said.

"That's great." Not exactly what I wanted to hear. "What did you find out?"

"He's got a pretty mahogany desk, a cedar credenza, coffeemaker, bathroom, closet, and a couple of nice watercolors on the wall. His filing cabinets even look like furniture. They're cedar or something, and--"

"I'm really and truly pleased as punch to hear the boy's done so well. So . . . what else did you find out?"

"You sound . . . jealous."

"Why? Because he drives a Lexus, has great furniture, and even owns a nifty coffeemaker?"

"His coffeemaker isn't so fancy. I like yours better."

I strongly suspected she was humoring me again.

"I like your office better, too."

"Why's that?"

"Because it's your office."

"Stop trying to make me feel better."

"Okay."

"And stop being so damned agreeable."

"Okay."

This was not going well at all.

"You sound mad."

"It's probably because I am."

"At me?"

"Of course not. I hate attorneys."

"I know."

"Rich people depress me."

"Maybe you should do something to get your mind off it."

"Like what?"

"Like going in there and upsetting him."

"I take it you didn't find anything in there."

"Sorry."

"No phone calls?"

"None."

"How about his calendar?"

"It's covered with scribblings, but I can't make anything out. It all looks like something a toddler would do if you handed them a pen."

"I think they learn that crap so they can write whatever they want without anyone else knowing what it is. Doctors do it, too. Anything on it for yesterday or this morning?"

"It looks like he's got something written for just about every day."

"Then something *was* there?"

"There's scribbling on it that looks like S-A-M, but I'm not even sure that's what it was."

"Sam?"

"I guess . . ."

I had to check it out. Getting him away from his desk was going to be my biggest challenge. It would be less tricky with Mike helping me.

"Um . . . before you go in?"

"Yes?"

"Please do something about your pooper face. You're so good-looking when you smile. Right now, you look like--well, like someone who's really constipated."

"I can't smile, Mike."

"Why not?"

"I'm about to see an attorney."

"So?"

"People who go to attorneys are usually in trouble. In other words, they aren't happy. If I go in there with a stupid grin on my face, he'll be suspicious."

"I guess you can keep your pooper face, then."

"See? I *knew* constipated would eventually come in handy."

Chapter Eight

The office was empty when we went in.

Like most strip mall offices, this one was long and narrow. A wooden coat rack stood just inside the door. Next to it, a dark-blue Armani jacket hung proudly and wrinkle-free on a polished silent butler.

On the other side of the door, a carved wooden pedestal stood near the wall. A yellowed antique powder horn rested on its surface.

About ten feet from the tinted glass storefront, a large mahogany desk sat angled toward the wall, facing the door. Two wide cushioned chairs faced the desk. A pricey-looking coffee station sat on the polished cedar credenza behind the desk.

In the center of the large area, a round cedar coffee table displayed three busts of Roman emperors. The busts were slightly smaller than actual human heads. I wasn't knowledgeable about Roman emperors, but I could recognize Julius Caesar when I saw him. I had no idea who the other two were. For all I knew, Caligula could have been one of them. Most corrupt, high-profile lawyers would admire a powerful nutcase.

Just beyond the coffee station, six cedar filing cabinets, each about four feet high, lined the eastern wall. About ten feet beyond them, two doors faced the front of the office. One was probably a closet, the other a bathroom.

"He's in the bathroom," Mike said.

Cool. I might have a few precious seconds to check his calendar. I took two steps toward the desk.

At that same moment, we heard the muffled sound of a flushing toilet.

"Quick. Check out the calendar before--"

The door eased open.

Kelly came out of the bathroom, straightening out his shirt collar and eyeing me curiously as I turned away from his desk.

The man was definitely not Italian. Since he was working for Papa Joe, I'd suspected he'd changed his name so he wouldn't be associated with Raguzzo. Shysters prefer not being associated with mobsters, doing whatever is necessary to remain detached from the crime element even though they make their big money working for thugs.

I hated to admit it, but Kelly was probably Irish. His neat, professionally styled reddish-brown hair and deep-set blue eyes could easily be a byproduct of the Emerald Isle. His tanned, closely shaven cheeks held no hint of stubble. Although caught without his jacket, he still looked sharp. His silk shirt, red cotton tie and silk blue slacks showed no wrinkles, and his tan Italian loafers glistened in the light from the small overhead fluorescent. He wore a sparkling Rolex. He also displayed a silver wedding band, and a gold horseshoe ring on the pinky of his right hand.

He looked like he belonged in a vodka ad with two sexy, half-dressed vixens hanging from him.

About forty years old, six feet tall, and around a hundred and seventy trim pounds, this boy had obviously seen serious breeding and education. The way he moved and how his eyes focused on me, summing me up at a glance, told me why Papa Joe had selected him. But it also told me I couldn't trust him. Those eyes were the kind that concealed much more than they expressed.

"May I help you?" His voice was soft and velvety, like the late actor, James Mason.

"That depends on who you are." I gave him back the same look of contemptuous distrust he was giving me and tried not to laugh when Mike drifted over to him and sniffed his cologne.

"My name's on the door. You would have most certainly seen it when you came in."

Touché. Cold and distant, and delivered with the same soft, velvety tone. This man could probably insult you, step outside, get in his car and drive off before you realized what he'd said.

Mike pulled away from him and wrinkled her nose. "Smells like imported perfume women use."

Kelly marched smartly over to his desk and stood between it and his fancy black leather chair. I figured two grand, easy, for the chair, close to five for the suit, twenty-five or so for the watch and jewelry, and another grand for those shoes.

"Then you must be Kelly, the attorney."

His gaze didn't waver. "I prefer *Mister* Kelly to people who don't know me. If you've come to retain my services, you may call me Dan or Daniel. Who might you be?"

"I'm Edward LeMans." Edward was the name of a favorite uncle who'd died when I graduated

105

from high school. He was Mom's little brother, and always teased me by talking to me in Italian. LeMans was the name of my favorite international raceway.

"Mr. LeMans." He held out his hand. I shook it and immediately wondered why all attorneys had oily hands. The handshake was brief and severe. He broke it off abruptly, nearly jerking it free--as if he was afraid my germs would transfer to his skin. He used the same hand to gesture to one of the chairs facing his desk. "Please. Have a seat. Would you like some coffee?"

"Don't mind if I do."

"What would you prefer?"

I forced myself to ignore that damned coffeemaker. The least I could do was get him to use it. It was probably a bear to clean. "What do you have?"

He gestured to it, his hands moving fluidly, like one of those models at a gadget convention. *Glide, don't walk. Be smooth. People are dazzled by eloquence, so give 'em what they want.* I expected him to give me a quick demonstration, flashing a glittering hero-smile before asking for questions from the audience. "We've got Irish cream, Cappuccino, vanilla, mint, mocha, raspberry--"

"How about a cup of good-ol' South American java?"

"No problem." He picked up a packet and went right to work. From the back he looked like a symphony conductor, coaxing the string section into a quiet *pizzicato* passage.

106

I moved my chair a little closer to the desk. The calendar was right there on his blotter, but upside-down, of course, and the scribbling was small as well as messy.

Mike was staring at one of the watercolors on the opposite wall. It was a black-and-white abstract of something that looked like a modernized horse head emerging from a kidney-shaped cloud hovering above a muddled group of stick buildings. I suspected that probably wasn't what it was, but it sure looked like it. It could be a blown-up ink blot Kelly had acquired from one of his nutcase clients, or perhaps a gift from a psychiatrist friend. I knew nothing about modern art, but judging by Kelly's expensive tastes, I figured the watercolor probably went for five or ten grand.

I tried getting Mike's attention, but as soon as I raised my left hand, Kelly turned and smiled. "Why'd you come to see me, Mister LeMans?"

"It's . . . about my wife."

Mike turned quickly, saw where I was looking, and drifted over. She lowered her face until her eyes were only a few inches from the calendar. A few seconds later, she looked up at me and shrugged.

Kelly turned back to his desk. "Coffee should be ready in about two minutes." He sat. "What about your wife, Mister LeMans?"

"We both want a divorce."

"And you'd like me to handle the details?"

"If I can afford you."

He smiled. "I'm sure we can come to some sort of amicable arrangement."

I smiled back. In attorney language, the term "amicable arrangement" meant, "I'm sure I can lower my standards and take payments even a lowlife like you can afford."

"Tell me a little about your situation."

"Such as?"

"Your profession. Background. Your wife's profession and background. Where do you and your wife live, for starters?"

"Well, that's a long story. . ."

The heavy aroma of Colombian coffee bubbling up from the coffee maker told me it was ready. The confined space quickly grew heavy with the strong scent.

Kelly placed his elbows carefully on the blotter. "I should think such a question could be answered simply, in just a few words, Mister LeMans. A simple address will do, actually." Kelly got up, turned, and picked up a clean cup from the credenza. He poured, then placed the cup and saucer on the desk, near the corner.

Now's a nifty time for a distraction, I thought, my focus on the calendar less than a foot away.

Kelly turned back to the credenza. He was grabbing the sugar and cream packets when I picked up the cup and spilled it on the floor, splashing the front of the desk, my chair, the other chair, and the toe of my right shoe.

"Dammit! Shit! I'm so *clumsy*!" I jumped up, carefully placing the empty cup back in its saucer. Then I pushed back the chair and searched my pockets for a Kleenex. "I guess my nerves are worse

108

than I thought, my wife stepping out on me and all. Let me mop up some of this spill while you get something from the bath--"

"It's quite all right." Kelly got up quickly.

I was about to pull out my cell while he rushed to the bathroom for towels. Instead, he'd opened a desk drawer, grabbed a thick roll of extra-strength Bounty paper towels and held it out.

"Uh, that's really terrific. Thanks." Sighing, I dropped to my knees and mopped up the spill. When I'd finished, I got back up, held the drenched towels in one hand and the roll in the other. He offered me his trash can. I wanted to offer him the heel of my shoe. I hated clever people--especially when they were rich. I dropped the filthy wet towels in it and he took the roll from me. His smile hadn't lowered a fraction of an inch. I wanted to smear his face with the towels, stuff them in his mouth, and punch him in the jaw. With my luck, his jaw was insured for a million bucks.

"Mind if I use your bathroom?" I held out my wet hands. "I need to wash." I also needed to talk to Mike about trying another tactic.

He gestured behind him. "Bathroom's the door on your left."

I crossed the room, slipped inside the small bathroom, flicked on the light and closed the door. Just as I turned on the faucet, Mike said, "He seems to be one step ahead of you."

"It's almost impossible to get the drop on a shyster--especially one who works for a mob boss."

"You work for one, too," she said.

She was right. I was just as smart as Kelly. I should be able to think of a way of getting what I needed.

"I'd make his phone ring," she said, "but he'll know something's not quite right."

"You can't act like you're a potential client?"

"How will that help you? He'll be at his desk, watching you, listening to me and hearing stereo."

I should have thought of that. "The calendar didn't tell you anything different this time around?"

"Just that SAM scrawl."

I dried my hands on the towels provided, turned off the light and left the room.

Kelly stood at his desk, facing me, that irritating smile still glowing. His left hand had moved away from his desk phone.

"Everything all right, Mister LeMans? Or should I call you Mister Deacon?"

I froze. He *had* made a call. "Uh, Deacon will do, but if you still want to call me LeMans, I'll--"

"You realize you've committed several misdemeanors, as well as a more serious crime I could use to revoke your license, should I choose to pursue this?"

"How'd you find out?"

"I have my sources."

"I'll bet you do."

"Then you won't mind if I decide to look into the small matter of checking your credentials to see if they are valid and up to date?"

I reached into my jacket pocket.

He shook his head. "Not exactly what I had in mind. But I appreciate the thought."

"Don't let him bully you," Mike said.

Kelly's smile brightened. "I happen to have friends in local government, Mister Deacon. Needless to say, we're all very concerned about questionable and suspicious practices of unscrupulous private detectives operating in the city of Orlando."

Questionable? Suspicious? From an attorney on retainer with a mob boss? Was this jerk for real?

Mike scooted over to his desk and gave the calendar another gander. She straightened about thirty seconds later and grinned. She'd obviously found something out.

"You are paying attention, are you not, Mr. Deacon?"

"Why do you ask?"

"You keep looking at my desk."

Mike stopped grinning. "It isn't *Sam* written there, it's five A.M. His five's all look like S's. I compared his chicken scratch with a couple of other dates and figured it out. Kind of a weird time for an appointment--wouldn't you say?"

I couldn't help it--I smiled.

"Something amusing?" Kelly asked.

"You could say that."

"Anyway, I intend to make a phone call once you leave. It'll be brief, I'm sure."

"Knock yourself out."

Kelly sighed. "Mr. Deacon, if I were you, I'd be a little worried."

I shrugged. "If I worried about everything, I wouldn't get any work done."

"I would think that your reputation--as well as your credentials--would be worth worrying about."

"Like I just said, I can't afford to worry. If I spent this afternoon worrying about what you're going to do, I wouldn't be able to do what I plan to do when I leave here."

Kelly's smile did not dim. "Whatever are you talking about?"

"I've got to do a little checking on my own. It concerns a client I'm working for. He's very successful and well-known around here, but right now he seems to be in a bind. He doesn't know who he can trust in his organization--which is kind of dangerous, considering the profession he's in."

Kelly's smile lowered a degree. "I don't see how this concerns--"

"I think you do. Someone like you knows exactly what's going on. And before you make that brief call about me, you might want to call someone else. The man I'm talking about would be a good bet. He's the one paying you two mill a year to fudge his taxes and whatever else he needs to keep the Feds off his butt. I'm sure he'll be happy to give you an accurate assessment of my credentials."

Kelly blinked.

"By the way, when you're talking to him, you might want to tell him I'll be getting in touch with him shortly. I've got to tell him what I learned about you."

Kelly was no longer smiling as I left his office.

Chapter Nine

Kelly didn't move as I got into the TransAm and backed out.

He continued watching me as he pulled his cell from his pocket. His antennae had been tugged loose, his thick attorney's hide scraped raw. I'd threatened him, forced him to defend himself. If I were a betting man, I'd say he was about to call Papa Joe, and probably forgot all about anyone else.

"Do you think that was wise?" Mike asked. "Mentioning your mob boss friend?"

"I'm not sure." I pulled out onto Semoran, crossing six lanes and heading south. "By the way, Raguzzo's not my friend."

"Why'd you do it?"

"He forced me. He also pissed me off, so I decided to shake his pedestal a little. I figured he wouldn't be tempted to make my life miserable if it meant threatening his profitable little setup with Raguzzo."

"Maybe that was okay, then. . ."

"Sometimes a gamble now and then actually works." I grabbed my cell and called Neil.

"Still alive?" he asked.

"No, this is my spiritual form drifting aimlessly in the atmosphere, bouncing ectoplasmic waves off one of the satellites--"

"Whaddya want, Deacon? I don't have time for your bullshit."

"Whose bullshit do you have time for?"

I heard him groan and decided I'd better state my business. Neil had no qualms about hanging up on me; he'd done it a few times before. And I usually had to apologize to get him to talk to me later on. I wasn't in the mood to apologize to anyone right now.

"Did you find out who sprung those two wet boys?"

"Ever hear of Louis Gallagher, of Gallagher, Gallagher, and Bundy?"

"Nope."

"It's a small local firm, and they handle taxes, wills, and some *pro bono* work for various charities. Their office is in the Central Florida Bank Building, on Orange and East Robinson."

"Shit." I'd hoped Kelly was the one involved. Now I had to work this from a different angle.

"I take it this doesn't help," Neil said.

"I was hoping it would be someone else, but at least now I've got a name to work with."

"You haven't seen them again, have you? Our wet boys?"

"It's only been two hours since I left your office."

"Well, keep your eyes open anyway. You know how this plays out. If you don't find them first--"

"I know. They'll find me."

"Ask him when those two were released," Mike said.

"Good idea."

"Howzat?" Neil asked.

"When were those two sprung?"

114

"Log says eight-thirty. Who were you talking to?"

"My conscience."

"You've done that before. It never helps."

"Maybe one day I'll surprise everyone and actually listen to it."

"I doubt that. Anyway, did that help?"

"Did what help?"

"The law firm, brainiac. Pay attention."

"Maybe, maybe not."

"Best I can do. But like I said, keep your eyes open."

"I will. And thanks."

"Eight-thirty isn't very close to five a.m.," Mike said as I pocketed my cell.

"You noticed that, too?"

"It's three and a half hours later."

"Noted."

"Maybe Kelly met Gallagher at five."

"Or maybe Gallagher went to see him."

"How's this? Kelly went to see them and paid them money to spring the two hitter guys. He then drove directly to his Orlando office while they went to the Police Station."

"Kelly's much too sly to work that way. He'd most likely move the money through PayPal or some other private account directly to their private account. Kelly deals with mob guys; he probably has a dummy company name he uses for personal purposes. In other words, there won't be a trail."

"Attorneys know one another, don't they?"

115

"I'm sure they move around in the same circles. There are separate classes for them. You've got public defenders, who work their asses off for a living, and another for the shysters like Kelly, who wear Armani suits, drive around in expensive rides and earn ginormous fees from rich mob guys who should be in prison."

"We have to find some way of tying Kelly in with this Gallagher firm."

"Even if we do, we still can't tie Kelly in with whoever's messing around with Papa Joe."

"Well, Kelly did *some*thing at five o'clock this morning. . ."

"We just don't know what," I said.

"Maybe one of the Gallagher's has something on their calendar we could use."

"Even so, we still can't pin this on Kelly."

"Look what he did as soon as you left the room. If that doesn't make him guilty of something, I don't know what does."

"He's an attorney, Mike. Attorneys are by nature suspicious--possibly because they're all crooks and consider everyone just as crooked as they are. There was probably something about me he didn't like, and as soon as I left the room, he made his call."

"How'd he work so fast? We were only in the john for two or three minutes."

"Kelly's been around the block a few times; he knows the drill. Three minutes was plenty of time for him to sneak outside, jot down my tag number, call his contact and run the number."

116

"But the DMV's always crowded. It was whenever I had to go there."

"Kelly's a VIP. If he was telling me the truth a few minutes ago and not just blowing smoke, he's got a ton of influential contacts. Someone like him can easily make a records clerk jump at the sound of his voice. In other words, he can have the clerk pull up someone else's files in less than a minute, while it would take a normal person like you or me half an hour to get the jerk to do the same thing."

"I'm not normal. I'm dead."

"I was trying to make a point."

"He *is* guilty, you know," she said.

"I know."

"The problem, as I see it, is proving it."

"Actually, the problem is finding out *what* he's guilty of--*then* proving it."

"Now I understand why you hate attorneys."

***

My cell buzzed just a few minutes later, as I turned off Colonial Drive and made a left onto Orange Avenue.

I recognized the harsh, Robert Loggia voice immediately. Papa Joe sounded even angrier than usual.

"Who the fuck you think you are, Deacon? You crazy or something?"

"Is that your mob boss friend?" Mike asked.

I turned away from the cell. "He's not my friend, but yeah, it's him."

"I'll bet he's mad."

"I'll bet you're right."

"You hear me, Deacon?"

"I hear you."

"Well? You crazy or what?"

"That's something a lot of people have been wondering for quite a while."

"Cut the shit. Where are you? And who the hell you pissing off now?"

"I'm in my car, driving along, minding my own business--"

"You went to see my attorney, you *sfachim*."

"Well, yeah, I--"

"I told you not to bother him."

"Well--"

"Didn't I tell you he's clean?"

"Well--"

"Didn't I tell you I've been using him for years?"

"Well--"

"And didn't I say I trust him?"

"Well--"

"What the fuck you got to say for yourself?"

"Well--"

"Can't you do better than that?"

"I'm trying to. . ."

"Then spit it out. What the hell's wrong with you?"

"Got a few minutes?"

A groan. "I ain't playing games, Deacon. You'd better tell me what the fuck you're doing, going behind my back to see my attorney and getting him all upset."

"He's upset?"

118

"You know he is, dammit!"

"Who's upset?" Mike asked.

"Kelly."

"Why should he be upset?" she asked. "You're the one who was threatened."

"Attorneys are all crazy. I thought you knew that."

"Deacon? Who the fuck you talking to?"

"Myself."

"Talk to *me*, *idiota*. *I'm* the one you got to worry about."

"Okay . . ."

"Whatta you got to say about that?"

"About what?"

"*Kelly*, dammit! You went to my attorney without my say-so and got him all upset!"

"Good. My work is done."

"Deacon, you *stronzone* . . . Listen to me, and listen good. I gave you good money to do a job for me. I didn't give you no money to stick your nose in my affairs and--"

"That's exactly why you gave me all that money."

Papa Joe sighed. "I didn't tell you to go snooping around, getting certain people all worked up."

"That's what I do. It's my business, and I do it well. If I wasn't so damned good at it, you wouldn't have hired me in the first place."

"Deacon, I told you, Kelly ain't involved."

"I hate to burst your bubble, but I don't think he's clean."

119

Silence. Then, in a softer voice: "You . . . find out something?"

"Not exactly. . ."

A groan. "Then what the fuck you talking about?"

"It's how he reacted to me."

"What the hell did he do?"

"It wasn't what he did, it was how he reacted when I went to see him."

"You think he's dirty 'cause he didn't act the way you wanted him to?"

"It was that, plus a couple of other things."

"Like what?"

"I can't explain it right now."

"I'm paying you twenty-five K for this, you know."

"I know. I was there when you offered it to me."

"That's a load of money."

"I know that, too."

"And now you're telling me you can't explain why you think Kelly is dirty?"

"Papa Joe, didn't you tell me you trusted me?"

"That don't mean you can go to my attorney and--"

"It means I can go to anyone if I think it'll get me the answers I need to find out what's going on in your organization."

A pause. "But . . . my *attorney*?"

"Maybe he isn't dirty. Maybe he is. What you need to understand is this. I have to find out, one way or another."

"You think you have something now?"

"I did find out a few things."

"But you don't know if he's dirty?"

"Not yet. . ."

"When will you know for sure?"

"Soon."

He sighed again, this time deeper. "Okay, Deacon. I'll letcha alone so you can do your job. But as soon as you find out about Kelly, I want to know quick--got it?"

"Got it."

"And if he *is* clean, I don't want you bothering him no more."

"There's no reason to--*if* he's clean."

"Keep me posted--*capire*?"

"Got it."

***

While Mike evaporated for another recharge, I eased into a parking space on Orange Avenue, less than a block south of the huge, glittering glass-and-concrete Central Florida Bank Building.

Instead of getting out, I stayed in the TransAm to work on my strategy. Every private eye expects the worst in every given situation, requiring him to have an ongoing backup plan. This way, when the worst happens, he stands a much better chance of getting away in one piece.

I had no positive proof that Kelly was dirty, but his paranoid reaction to my visit strongly suggested he had something to hide. There was no other explanation for his phone call about me. If I was right, he knew about the two hitters. Whether or not he'd hired them didn't matter. If he was involved, he knew exactly what I was up to and who I was looking for and had already warned the Gallaghers about me. They'd be expecting me and would have their alibis ready.

The alibis wouldn't matter. They'd gotten two professional hitters out of jail. I knew all about the Constitution . . . and the right to have legal representation . . . and the innocent-until-proven-guilty thing . . . and most everything else protecting our personal freedoms . . .

What mattered to me was that two professional hit men were now wandering around free, and the law firm responsible for their freedom kept offices in the building just a hundred feet down the street.

The thoughts of two hit men looking for me made the back of my neck heat up. But even in my stressed state, I realized I couldn't just walk in there and ask them about it. Attorneys didn't discuss their business with anyone; it was against their professional code of ethics. I'd only infuriate them, as I'd done with Kelly.

Once again I had to rely on Mike. I had no choice but wait in the car while she went in and did the dirty work. As she'd done in Kelly's office, she could check out their calendars to see if anything was written for last night or this morning. She could also drift in and out of the offices, listening for juicy conversation. If she didn't learn anything incriminating, I'd ask her to ride home with one of them at the end of the day and get back to me later on.

I glanced at the dash clock. One-fifteen.

I suddenly realized I'd skipped lunch entirely. No wonder my stomach had been making weird sounds.

Once Mike reappeared, I'd find the closest takeout place and grab a cheeseburger, then come back and wait for her.

I glanced at the empty seat beside me.

"Mike?"

No response.

I sat back in the seat and closed my eyes.

Someone tapped on my passenger window.

A skinny young babe with long blond hair brought her face close to the window. She wore a red visor and large, red-tinted sunglasses, and was darkly tanned in her sleeveless yellow tank top. She motioned for me to roll down the window.

I hesitated. Something didn't feel right.

She pointed straight ahead, down the street, and said something, but the traffic sounds made it impossible for me to hear her.

She was cute, even sexy for a small-breasted babe . . . but I still didn't feel comfortable.

She shook her head and pointed again. She was definitely upset about something.

I lay across the seat and rolled down the window. As soon as I did, the driver's door squealed open behind me. I jerked my head around.

A tall, gangly young guy with long, greasy brown hair and full beard leaned inside. He wore a black Greek yachting cap, a black leather vest, and faded jeans. A small black automatic grew out of his hand like a bruised knuckle. It was pointed at my gut.

"Slide over," he said flatly.

Dammit. Why do I have to be right all the time?

Minding the console, I pushed myself up and did as he said.

He got behind the wheel. The blonde opened the back door and climbed in behind us. He slammed the driver's door and handed her the gun, which she pressed firmly against the back of my neck.

"What's this all about?" I asked.

"Shuddup." Beard fired up the TransAm and squealed out of the spot.

Chapter Ten

Beard kept with the flow, riding the brakes, and switching lanes without warning.

I wanted to tell him to ease up. I didn't want to pay for a brake job so soon after I'd replaced the compressor. But the gun pressed against the back of my neck had made me reluctant to voice my opinion.

Beard roared through a red light and switched lanes, cutting off an SUV. The angry driver punched his horn and kept it blaring for several seconds. Beard retaliated by calling him an asshole and flipping him the bird.

Terrific. I'd just been kidnapped by two idiots. Needless to say, the realization didn't make me feel any better.

"Can't leave you for a moment, can I?" Mike appeared in the back, on Blondie's left. I couldn't move my head but could see her shape out of the corner of my eye. In spite of the gun pressing into my neck, I sighed in relief. Things were about to get interesting.

"Nope," I told Mike.

"Shuddup," Beard barked.

"Not very nice, are they?" Mike said.

I knew better than reply. I had the uneasy feeling Blondie had never used a gun before. People who don't know about guns are much more dangerous--especially when they've got one and are pressing it against someone's neck.

Beard made a sharp right onto West Central Boulevard. My pulse began racing. There was much less traffic on this stretch. Less witnesses. My paranoia thundered back.

We went several blocks west, through a section lined with warehouses, storage buildings and abandoned garages.

I could tell we weren't driving to my favorite section of Orlando, but I didn't want to ask about it. Blondie might accidentally pull the trigger and alter my future entirely.

The automatic was very small and compact, no doubt a .22. This intensified my fears. I wasn't fond of having a gun pointed at me *at all*, and dreaded this caliber more than any other. You can get shot in the neck at close range with a .22 and survive. You'd be alive but paralyzed from the neck down.

I longingly thought of my .380 lying in the console, so close to my grasp . . .

About twenty minutes later, Beard turned left onto Orange Blossom Trail. We went south, toward an even seedier section of town. I wondered who they were working for, where they were taking me and what they intended to do once we got there. I suspected this wasn't a simple carjacking. The area where they'd nabbed me was mostly corporate, and not common for carjackings. I suspected Kelly or the Gallagher's had gotten together and paid these two to take me out of the picture.

To test them, I shrugged to get the blood flowing in my shoulders and neck, and was rewarded by a swat to the back of the head. "Don't move, asshole," Blondie whispered close to my ear, and I caught a whiff of her mouthwash and perfume. The perfume had a sandalwood aroma--which I was fond of--but I was much too scared and angry for it to have any effect.

"Just working out the kinks," I said.

She swatted me again, in the same place. "Don't move. And don't talk."

"She's not a nice lady," Mike said. "I think she needs to be uncomfortable."

I wanted to smile.

Blondie suddenly reached up with her free hand and rubbed her ear. "*Damm*it. . ."

"Now for the driver," Mike said.

"What the *fuck*--" He swatted his right ear, and the TransAm swerved sharply, bumping the curb.

"Watch it, baby!" Blondie wrapped her free arm around the headrest. The pressure on my neck eased up.

"Couldn't help it," he growled. "Something stung me in the fucking ear!"

"Something got me, too. But watch it. We can't spend the money dead, ya know." The pressure on my neck increased.

I was right. This wasn't a carjacking.

"Fuck you," he said. "I can handle this ride." He suddenly gasped and slapped the back of his neck. The big car swerved again, and we almost sideswiped the cream-colored sedan beside us. "What the fuck is *in* this wreck?" He gawked toward the back. "Mosquitoes? Horseflies?"

"Who knows?" The pressure eased up on my neck once again. "This thing's a hundred years old. It's prob'ly got shit from the Civil War slithering around in the upholstery."

My fear evaporated. It was one thing to jack my car and stick a gun in my neck. But when my classic ride was criticized, I had to draw the line.

"This car's a classic," I said.

"I told you to shut up, asshole!" Blondie swatted me again.

I gasped and doubled up.

"Now I'm *really* getting angry," Mike said.

"I think you need a nap, Slick." Beard reached into his vest pocket.

Mike zapped him again, this time on the back of the head. He jerked to his left. The TransAm swerved, bumping the island in the middle lane. The pressure on my neck disappeared as Blondie jerked to her right, slamming against the side window.

I turned sharply and groped for the gun, but Blondie had already regained her balance. She steadied the gun in her hands and pulled back the hammer.

Mike zapped her again. Cringing, Blondie squealed, turned her head, and reached behind her. "What the fuck is *back* there?"

I snatched the gun and aimed it at Beard just before his fist emerged from his pocket, gripping a set of brass knuckles. I grabbed his wrist, leaned forward and pressed the gun against the side of his neck. "Pull over," I said. "Now."

He kept on driving, increasing speed as we went through another red light. "You can't get us both," he said, a sneer on his face.

"You're right. Mike? Zap her again."

Blondie pulled away, squealed and began scratching her scalp vigorously with both hands. Keeping the gun on Beard's neck, I flipped open the console, grabbed the .380, pulled back the hammer and pointed it directly at his right eye.

"This work better for you?"

Beard's eyes bulged. He gulped audibly. "M-Mike? Z-Zap? Huh? Wh-What? Who--"

"Stop making those silly noises. You sound like a nervous chimpanzee. And drop the fake knuckles on the floor. Right now."

His hand shaking, he did as ordered. It bounced off the hump on the floor and slid toward my left foot. I covered it with my shoe and kept the .22 buried in his neck. I then lowered the .380 and shoved it into his crotch, driving a gasp from him. "You wanna pull over? Or would you like to watch your nuts turn into Jell-O first?"

He trembled, his fists turning white as they gripped the wheel. "M-Mister--"

"Shut up and pull over." I pushed the barrel harder into his crotch. He yelped, jumping in the seat.

I eased up on the pressure and he stopped squirming. He slowed down, put on his blinkers, eased into the right lane and pulled into the side lot of a shopping center. He went another twenty feet or so, then stopped. Luckily, we were more than a hundred feet from the closest shoppers and parked vehicles.

As soon we'd stopped moving, I said, "Put it in park and turn off the ignition."

Again, he complied.

"Remove the keys with your left hand and drop them on the floor on my side."

Once again, he obeyed.

"Lean forward and place the bridge of your nose on the wheel."

"B-But--"

"I told you about the stuttering. Now shut up and do the steering wheel thing."

With a deep sigh, he did as I ordered.

"Put your hands behind your back. And if I even feel Bonnie Parker moving around back there, you can say bye-bye to your family jewels. Hear me back there?"

Silence.

"I said--"

A groan. "I hear you . . ."

Beard was shaking. "B-But we j-just did this for--"

"I didn't tell you to talk." I cracked him on the side of the head with the .22, and he grunted. "Now . . . do what I just told you or I'll do the same thing again."

He pulled his arms behind his back.

"Now lean back against the seat."

Again, he obeyed.

I kept the .380 on his face and the .22 trained on Blondie. "I've got something for your girlfriend to do, and she'd better do it exactly the way I tell her. If she doesn't, I'm gonna be very upset. In case you don't know this already, you really don't want to upset someone who's holding two loaded guns on you. Get it?"

Beard's face paled as he nodded.

"Get it, lady?"

She gulped as if she'd just swallowed something unpleasant. Her skin turned blotchy just below her breastbone. She just wasn't comfortable without her little toy. "Listen, Mis-Mister . . . w-we d-didn't--"

"I *said*, you got it?"

She groaned softly. "I got it. . ."

"I'm glad we're all onboard." Watching them both, I put the .22 in my lap and transferred the .380 to my left hand. Keeping it trained on Beard, I reached underneath the seat and found a knot of bungee cords I keep on hand for emergencies. I've used them to fasten things in the trunk but haven't used them on people yet. I figured they'd be good enough. I grabbed a three-foot-long blue one and handed it to Blondie. "Put this on your boyfriend."

She blinked. "That's a *bungee cord*."

"Thanks. You've got good eyes. Now . . . put it on him."

"*On* him? Where?"

"You can't be serious."

She just shrugged.

"I think she's serious," Mike said.

"I'm gonna make this simple. I'll even talk slow." I tapped Beard's shoulder with the .380.

131

"Lean forward and rest your nose against the steering wheel. And keep your arms behind your back. One wrong move and I use this gun to tap the back of your head."

He trembled while carefully lowering his face.

I gestured to Blondie. "Tie his wrists and do it right."

She wrinkled her nose. "With a *bungee cord*?"

Her stupidity was wearing thin. "It's all I seem to have with me. I wasn't planning on tying up anyone today. I usually save that for Friday afternoons, when I can't get a date and shop for one at Bally, The Nail Shoppe, or the local high school."

"The local high school?" Mike asked.

"I was on a roll," I told her.

"Good. I wondered."

Beard turned and squinted. "What, man?"

"Just talking to my imaginary friend." I turned to Blondie. "Anyway, unless you've got something better in mind, wrap that around his wrists and use the hooks to fasten it."

With shaky fingers she applied the loops to Beard's wrists and let the hooks hang.

"It's no good unless you fasten it."

She hooked it loosely.

"I need it tighter."

She froze. Apparently she couldn't wrap her tiny mind around the concept.

"She's confused," Mike said.

"Obviously."

"Huh?" Blondie asked.

132

"My imaginary friend just voiced her opinion and I agreed. Listen. And please try to understand the situation. I don't want him to get free. I might as well just give you back your gun and let you two take me wherever you were taking me. Does that make any sense?"

Carefully she ran another loop around his wrists and hooked it clumsily. It would work for now, but I'd redo it once I had her fixed.

"Now turn around, pull your arms back, and rest them over the top of the seat."

She did it reluctantly, kneeling on the edge of the back seat.

"Put your hands together and interlace your fingers."

She reluctantly complied.

I slipped another long bungee around her wrists and hooked it tightly. She squealed, arching her back. "That *hurts*!"

"That's what I mean by tight." I raised her arms a little and pushed her into the back seat. She landed with a grunt, her visor coming off, her sunglasses shifting down onto her nose.

"Brute," Mike said.

I checked the loops around Beard's wrists and yanked it tighter, driving a harsh grunt from him. "*Now* it's tight enough." I grabbed him by the collar and pushed him back against the seat.

"Whatta ya g-gonna d-do to us, Mac?" he whispered hoarsely.

"I haven't given it much thought. And my name ain't Mac."

"This is fucked up, man. Really fucked up."

"I'll say it is. You messed up my afternoon. Now I've got to mess up yours. It's kind of like when you punch someone. Unless you were lucky enough to knock him out, he's *gotta* punch you back. It's that Karma thingy. It can be a real bitch."

"P-*Please*, Mister . . ." Blondie decided on the sweet and humble approach.

It was amazing how quickly a girl's attitude changed when you took her gun away from her.

"Please what?"

"P-Please don't . . . don't k-kill us. I'll let you d-do anything you w-want . . ."

"Anything?"

"Anything. You don't even have to . . . untie me."

"What a deal," Mike said flatly.

"You mean you'd do an old guy like me?"

She nodded eagerly. Her glasses fell off, landing on the seat beside her.

I glanced at Beard. "That all right with you?"

He stared straight ahead. "Fuck yeah. If it gets us outa this . . ."

I turned back to Blondie. "As tempting as that sounds, I'm really not in the mood."

Her eyes grew. "Please? Anything you want."

"That sure is a dynamite offer, but I'm gonna have to pass. When someone steals my car, jams a gun into my neck and swats me on the back of my head, I just can't get worked up too much below decks, if you know what I mean."

"*Please*, Mister . . ."

134

Beard just shook his head. "Really fucked up, man."

"Turn toward me and put your feet on the seat, over the console."

"Dude? Can't ya just drop us somewhere and--"

"Maybe later. Right now? Do as I say. And my name ain't Dude."

With a deep groan, he heaved them up. When his scuffed black shit-kickers landed on the seat, I looped another long bungee around his ankles and pulled it tight.

"Put them back down."

Once again he complied.

I took another bungee and got out. No one was within earshot but the passing traffic. I opened the back door. Blondie hadn't budged in the back seat. Her visor was pointed straight up. She was glaring, but pale with fear. Mike sat beside her, watching me. I motioned for Blondie to place her legs on the seat. When she did, I tightly bound her ankles.

"Please fix her visor and glasses," Mike urged. "It makes her look, well, silly."

"Sure wouldn't want that, would we?" I did as Mike suggested. Blondie watched me closely, her big blue eyes on me, her lower lip all pouty and pushed out. If she hadn't pissed me off so much, I might have taken her up on her offer. But there were more important issues here. I wasn't about to ignore what they'd just tried to do to me.

I slammed the back door and circled the car, opened the driver's door and motioned to Beard with my gun. "Scoot over."

Beard had trouble negotiating his long frame over the console, but he managed. I got behind the wheel, closed the door and picked up my keys. "Everyone cozy?"

Beard said nothing. Blondie made a sound like a frightened bird.

I started up the ignition.

"Wh-Where you . . . t-taking us, man?" Beard asked softly.

"It's a surprise."

He swallowed loudly and mashed himself against the door.

I turned toward the back, where Mike was sitting beside Blondie. Both women looked frightened. "That goes for you, too. Understand?" I asked Blondie.

Blondie nodded.

Mike trembled. "*I* sure do."

"Oh, stop it." Despite my burning anger, it was an effort to keep from laughing. I gave Beard another glare just for the hell of it, laid the .380 in my lap, fired up the ignition and pulled out into the southbound traffic.

Chapter Eleven

My two prisoners kept silent as I drove.

I figured they'd both wet their pants if I picked up my gun and cocked the hammer. That would be hilarious, but I didn't want my seats messed up.

These two were amateurs. Kids. Someone had paid them to dump me somewhere. To them, this was an adventure, a hoot. I didn't think either of them had the balls to do me in, but these days, you couldn't tell.

But I had to find out.

A few miles later, as we passed a row of outrageously-painted buildings and half a dozen street corner hookers, I knew we'd reached the right neighborhood. Small groups of young black men in loose-fitting sweatshirts, baggy pants pulled down to their knees, and athletic shoes shuffled down the street, chattering away.

It was nearly a quarter to two, and the lunch hour traffic was still going strong. As we passed the gaudy purple, yellow and pink buildings, their packed parking lots clearly confirmed the business volume this trade handled. Many of the vehicles were high-priced rides.

"You gonna k-kill us, man?" Beard asked in a soft voice.

"Shut up."

"Please, Mister," Blondie whimpered from the back.

"You, too."

"You're being *so* mean," Mike said. "Untie her and give her back her gun. She'll feel *so* much better."

I laughed.

"You okay, man?" Beard regarded me uneasily.

"I tend to get a little crazy when someone jacks my car and kidnaps me. And the gun-to-the-back-of-my-neck thing rubbed me the wrong way, too."

"It was . . . it was for *money*, Mister--"

"He doesn't wanna hear it, baby."

"How much?" I asked.

"Don't matter," Beard said. "Not now."

I sighed. "How much?"

"T-Two hundred," she said.

"Two *hundred*?" I couldn't believe it.

"Apiece," Blondie added.

"Ah. Well then, that makes *much* more sense."

"Really?" Blondie asked.

"No. You're both idiots."

These two were much stupider and more naïve than I'd originally thought.

I reached into my pocket and pulled out my cell.

"Who you . . . wh-who you c-callin', man?" Beard whispered.

"A friend. He's a cop at OPD. Why?"

"*Please* don't call the cops!" Blondie struggled to sit up.

"Please, man!" Beard pleaded. "It was just . . . he paid us two hundred apiece . . . just to--"

"Who paid you?"

Silence.

I pressed two buttons.

138

"He told us not to tell anyone!" Blondie practically shouted.

"Of course he told you that. If he'd paid you to do this and tell everyone about it, would you have been stupid enough to do it?"

Silence. Hopefully they were activating some brain cells they hadn't used in a while.

I pressed another button.

"His name's Al-Albert," Blondie said.

I stopped pressing buttons. "That's got a nice ring to it."

"Everyone calls him B-Berto," she said.

"Go on."

"He . . . he runs a place on Orange."

"Orange goes on forever. A gazillion places on it, last I checked. You'll have to do better."

"About a block north of East Concord."

"That helps. Now . . . . what kind of place?"

"Used bookstore."

Somehow I couldn't wrap my tiny brain around a shady character running a used bookstore. A pit bull breeder, maybe. Or even a gun store owner with a neo-Nazi setup in the back of the store. But a used bookstore?

"You're not serious."

"He's been there for years." Blondie was earnest.

"I take it he's not young."

"He's old," Beard said.

"Real old," Blondie added.

"How old?"

"Forty or so," Beard said. "Maybe fifty."

"About your age," Blondie said.

Mike gasped. "Oh, no . . ."

"Guess what? I've just decided to shoot both of you." I grabbed the .380 in my lap.

"Please don't, man!"

Blondie began whimpering again.

"I've got to find a dumpster first. Then I won't have to worry about the cleanup."

Blondie's whimpers grew in pitch.

"Please, man!" Now Beard looked like he was about to cry.

"Oh, shut up, both of you." I put the gun back in my lap and stopped at the red light. I needed to dump these two idiots somewhere. They'd cost me too much time. But I needed to find out more.

"This really old, decrepit, forty-year-old geezer. Berto. What's he look like?"

"Long white hair," Beard offered. "Messy."

"Real messy," Blondie added. "Like Einstein."

"How do you know him?"

"We were in one of his classes."

"Classes?" This was getting even more bizarre.

"College. You know."

"Ah, yes. College. Every once in a while, when my Alzheimer's fades away for a few precious moments, my thoughts actually turn lucid, and I fondly remember the old days, before the automobile, computers, TV, space travel and cell phones."

Their silence told me they had no idea what I was talking about.

"They're young," Mike said.

140

"Stupid, too. The fact that they've been to college really scares me."

Beard eyed me suspiciously again.

"Old people talk to themselves a lot," I explained.

He nodded.

"This Berto . . . you say he's a college professor?"

"Just a few classes in the summer. English lit, mostly."

"And he runs a bookstore and hands out a little wet work on the side?"

"Wet work?" Blondie sounded confused.

"We weren't supposed to kill you, man," Beard said.

"Just what *were* you supposed to do?"

He shrugged. "Take you somewhere."

"Where?"

"Somewhere around here."

"Then what?"

"Lock you in your trunk."

"And then?"

"Walk away."

"You're kidding, right?"

Beard shrugged. So did Blondie. They were obviously telling the truth. I was right about them being morons.

"Just lock me in my trunk and walk away?"

"We were supposed to leave the keys in the ignition," Beard said. "Nothin' else, I swear."

"Someone was supposed to come and take you away," Blondie said.

"Who?"

"Berto never said," Beard replied. "We both figured it would be him. He told us to get away as soon as we left the keys."

The plan was vicious, and these two apparently didn't see anything wrong with it. Two hundred bucks apiece, just for taking me into a bad section of town and leaving me locked in the trunk. An hour of their time, tops. What could be sweeter?

"You kidnapped me at gunpoint. You also stuck an automatic into my neck and slapped me around. You scared me half to death."

"I'm sorry, Mister. . ."

"I know you are. What's Berto's last name?"

"Shields."

That was all I needed. I picked up the cell and spoke into it. "Got all that, Mike?"

"Cute," she said.

"Yeah," I said to the empty line, "I have them both right here. I managed to get the gun from the blonde." I paused again. "Sure, if you think we have all we need." I snapped the cell shut and pocketed it.

"Who-Who was that?" Beard asked nervously.

"Oh, just someone at the Police Station taping our conversation."

Blondie began whimpering again. I cursed myself for not having a spare sock to stuff into her big mouth. It would be tacky and time-consuming to pull over, take off one of my shoes and shove the sock down her throat. I fought down the urge. I didn't like the feel of wearing a shoe without the

142

sock. And I certainly didn't want to put it back on after it had been soaking in her sorry mouth.

I pulled onto a residential street and cruised halfway down the block, until we came to a deserted lot. A dilapidated block garage stood in the center, its blocks cracked and green from the elements, its wide aluminum door ripped off the track, with half of it lying on the slab like a collapsed shower curtain. Grass and weeds grew wild, obscuring sections of its walls and a portion of its front. I eased down the overgrown drive and stopped about ten feet from the gaping doorway.

"What . . . what're you g-gonna do . . . with us?" Blondie's trembling lips gave me the impression she was about to scream. It would undoubtedly be blood-curdling.

I reached down and unhooked the bungee around Beard's ankles. Then I got out, circled the car and opened the back door. After reaching in and freeing Blondie's ankles, I pointed to the doorway. She didn't move, so I grabbed her by the belt and pulled.

"If I have to haul you out by your ankles," I said, "it's gonna really ruin your day when your head slams down onto the concrete and cracks open."

"I don't . . . wanna . . . die," she gasped.

I turned to Beard, who sat in the seat, staring straight ahead. "I know she's skinny and hot and all, but she's a major pain in the ass."

He nodded.

"She must pull chrome, right?"

143

He sighed and nodded again.

"You're mean," Mike said flatly. "And so crude . . ."

"Tell me something I don't know." I turned back to Blondie. "I'm not gonna kill you."

She stared wildly at me behind the red-tinted shades, her skin breaking out in red blotches again.

"She doesn't believe you," Mike said.

"I got that." I stared at Blondie and tried my best not to glare. It was tough; she was really pissing me off. "Please get out, okay? I've got things to do this afternoon."

"You're gonna . . . k-kill us . . . aren't you?"

"I just said I'm not. Now . . . please get out. I don't have all day."

"I don't want . . . why'd you even bring us here?"

"The Hilton's booked solid. They probably wouldn't let us stay there, anyway; we don't have any luggage. Besides, the bungee cords would make them suspicious."

"This place . . ." She wrinkled her nose. "It's . . . filthy here. . ."

I gave Beard another sympathetic glance. He was shaking his head.

"Maybe if *you* tell her to get out," I said.

"Patsy, get out, like the man says."

After another lengthy pause, she squirmed on the seat. I grabbed her upper arm and helped her out, then opened the passenger door. Beard got out on his own, and I followed them inside the dark garage, between piles of boxes and stacked junk. The smell was rancid, reeking of mold, cigarette smoke and motor oil. Roaches and mice scurried everywhere. Blondie squealed, sidestepping, jumping, hopping and pressing against Beard, nearly knocking him down. "*Ick!* Why are we here?" she whispered, wrinkling her nose.

"Because you pissed me off, and I want this experience to be the last of its kind in your budding careers as young criminals."

"Huh?"

"We won't do this again, man," Beard said.

"Do you realize what would've happened if you had locked me in that trunk and walked away?"

They both gave me that glazed, deer-in-the-headlights look. They were either trying to look innocent or were genuine morons.

"Let me paint you a clearer picture. A locked trunk? In a black car? In Central Florida? With no air? Even in the spring on a cool day, the temperature inside that trunk's liable to hit a hundred and thirty degrees."

Blondie's glazed look did not change.

"We're done with this, man." There were tears in Beard's eyes. I guessed he'd finally realized the seriousness of the situation.

Even so, I wanted to knock their heads together to see if any recognizable brain matter trickled out.

"I've got the two of you on tape. And just so we understand one another, if I see either of you again, I will kill you." I took the .380 out of my waistband. "With this." I pointed it at both of them.

Beard swallowed audibly and looked down. Blondie scrunched up her face and turned sharply away.

With my free hand, I unhooked the bungee binding Blondie's wrists. She could unhook her boyfriend. Then, watching my step, I backed up, until I was outside. "You both have cell phones?"

They nodded.

"Good. Call someone if you want to get out of here, all right?"

Beard nodded. Blondie was still staring at my gun.

"See how nice I am?" I slid the .380 down my waistband. "I not only didn't kill either of you, but I let you keep your cell phones, too. And people actually think there are no more good guys left."

"You really are sweet," Mike said.

"Just a sucker. And by the way, if I find out either of you tipped off Berto, I'm gonna make a quick trip to OPD, look up my friend Mike, and make copies of the tape to hand out to the cops. Its contents will nail you for conspiracy to commit murder, kidnapping, unlawful imprisonment, depraved indifference, assault and battery--and, of course, car theft. That adds up to . . . let's see . . . I figure around life for both of you--or maybe just twenty years apiece, if you get a kindly judge. Got it?"

They both nodded eagerly.

I went back to the TransAm.

"Mister?" Blondie called.

"Now what?"

Her face was wet with tears, her makeup smeared and runny around her shades. "Thanks."

"Just don't do this again. To anyone. The next guy might not be a good guy at all." Then I got back into the TransAm.

"That was sweet," Mike said. "Very touching."

"A real Kodak moment." I backed out of the space and drove down the street.

"Where are we going?"

"I haven't been to a bookstore in a while."

Chapter Twelve

SHIELDS BOOKS (*"If we don't have it, it hasn't been written yet!"*) faced the Orlando *Sentinel* Building.

Sandwiched between a tropical fish store and a place selling tee shirts, leather jackets and exotic pets, the bookstore was small and narrow, with a green awning hiding part of the smudged window. A pyramid of dusty First Editions provided the storefront display, with a plaster bust of William Shakespeare sitting in front, looking bored as he watched the front door.

At two-fifteen, I pulled into the parking lot of the *Sentinel* and found a spot in the first row, between a silver Honda Accord and a canary-yellow VW. I killed the ignition, lowered the window, and stared at the bookstore directly across the street, just above the trimmed bushes lining the front of the lot.

"What are you doing?" Mike asked.

"I'm thinking."

"Again?"

"Scary, huh? Twice in one day."

"Not really—just so you don't decide to do something stupid."

"Like what?"

"Walking into the bookstore and showing him your gun."

"I'm not even gonna take my gun with me."

"What are you going to do, then?"

"I'm not sure. That's why I'm not getting out."

"I could go in and sniff around, if you like."

"I just don't know what any of this will accomplish. Going by what those two idiots said, Shields paid them to kidnap me. That doesn't tell me anything about Papa Joe's organization. Or who the traitors are."

"Maybe all you have to do is find out why he paid them. Then everything else will fall into place."

"It really bothers me that this jerk paid two kids to do that."

"It could've been worse."

I couldn't believe she'd said that. "How do you figure?"

"They could've been paid to kill you."

"To them, it was just a game. They park the TransAm in a bad section of town and walk away. And while they're spending their money on something stupid, I'm lying in my trunk, suffocating. What do you mean, it could've been worse?"

"They didn't get to do it, did they?"

"Only because you stopped it."

She smiled.

"Now that we're on the subject, how the hell did you get them to scratch themselves like that?"

She shrugged. "I just focused and thought, Pins and needles, needles and pins."

"Cool. Some phrase right out of a bad Santa Claus flick saved my ass."

"I'm just glad it worked."

"I knew there was a good reason why I always liked Christmas so much. So . . . all I have to do is figure out what to do here."

"Do you think this Berto guy might be a member of the Mob?"

"He obviously knows the Gallagher's. That by itself doesn't tell me much. But it does tell me he's bad."

"Doesn't it imply the Gallagher's could be involved with those hit men?"

"The fact that they sprung the two only means they were paid to do it. For all we know, someone at OPD might have told them about it, and they did it as a favor. Neil did say they do *pro bono* work. If they did it, it doesn't tell me why, or who paid them. I still have no idea who those two hitters were."

"How can you find out about this Shields guy without scaring him like you scared the two college kids?"

"That's what friends are for." I pulled out my cell and punched the key for Neil.

He answered on the first ring. "I'm busy, Deacon."

"Do me a large favor."

"I don't have the time."

"It'll only take you a few minutes."

He sighed. "Make it fast."

"Look up Albert Shields and tell me if he's got a sheet."

"Now why would I want to do that?"

"Let's just say I have a feeling about him."

A pause. "Think this character might be tied in with those two wet boys?"

"I'm not sure. That's why I need to find out about him."

Another pause. "I'm in the middle of something right now. Gimme ten minutes."

"Thanks." I put the cell on the console.

"Want me to go on in and nose around?" Mike asked.

"You probably won't find anything."

"It never hurts to try."

"I'll be here when you get back."

"You're not gonna tell me to be careful?"

"You ought to do standup."

I could hear her laughing even after she'd disappeared.

***

While Mike was gone, I considered crossing the street and heading down to the end of the block, to the local supermarket.

Since I no longer faced an agonizing death in the hot trunk of my classic car, my priorities had changed, and the emptiness in my gut made itself known once again.

I decided to hold off until I found out what was going on in the bookstore. I considered walking inside to see what Mike was doing. My thoughts quickly turned to fantasy, and I saw myself as Philip Marlowe in *The Big Sleep*, approaching the female clerk and asking her about a *Ben Hur* 1860 First Edition, with that duplicated line on page 116.

In my fantasy, Shields' clerk, like the one in the Chandler story, was ash blonde, with green eyes and beaded lashes. Her nametag said *LILA*, and her long legs showed prominently in her tight black dress. She looked me up and down, told me there was no such First Edition, then spun around and sashayed back to the counter. Her Marilyn Monroe-style walk suggested Jell-O-on-springs. A different story, but my imagination knew no bounds.

My cell buzzed. It was Neil, forcing me back to reality.

"Found a few things," he said. "Petty stuff, but enough to give you a little something about this Shields character."

"I'm listening."

"Albert Louis Shields, age fifty-seven."

Fifty-seven? Blondie thought Shields and I were the same age. I should have tortured both for an hour or two. Their colossal stupidity should come with a hefty price.

"Shields is a native, born in the Miami area. Went to the University of Miami, majored in English Lit. Taught for a year or so before he got caught up in the peace movement. He was arrested for a slew of things--unlawful assembly, public nuisance, pot-smoking, some hashish--"

"This was during Vietnam, I take it?"

"You got it. Nothing big, as I said earlier."

I waited for him to go on. He didn't.

"That's it?"

"It was. Until recently."

"How recently?"

152

"Apparently Shields never got over his drug addiction. He was charged with cocaine possession twice in the last six months."

"In Miami?"

"Orlando, the first time. The other bust was last month, in Biloxi."

"Biloxi? Mississippi?" This was getting interesting.

"You always were good at geography, Deacon."

"I can also crush a beer can with one hand and belch on cue."

"At the same time?"

"When my biorhythm's on the upswing. So tell me what happened with that Biloxi bust."

"Shields was sprung within two hours."

Strange. "What are the details in the report?"

"He was at one of the casinos when a house cop caught him snorting in the men's room."

"Which casino?"

"It says the Coastal Grande."

I'd heard the Coastal Grande was mob-owned. This was getting interesting. "Got the name of the guy who bailed him out?"

"Sid Raymer. He's a local bail bondsman up there."

I got out my little notebook and started scribbling.

"Deacon?"

"When exactly did this happen last month?"

"Middle of the month."

This was getting better and better.

"That all you need?"

"That's helpful, Neil. Thanks."

"You won't mind, then, if I get back to my other job? The one where I'm actually paid?"

"Be my guest." I hung up and called Vesper's. I asked the sweet thing who answered to get me Sonny Bergman.

"Whaddya want, Deacon?"

"I need to talk to your boss."

"This line bugged?"

Sonny was beginning to sound like Papa Joe. All he needed was to swallow some ground glass, add thirty years to his age, lose his hair and drop about a hundred and fifty pounds. "No, it's not bugged. Tell him I have to talk to him ASAP." Then I hung up.

Mike materialized beside me, this time in her low-necked short-sleeve red blouse, tan Capri's, and open-toed brown pumps. I loved Mike in Capri's. She had sensational calves.

"Stop along the way to change?" I asked.

"Just before I came back. Is it okay?"

"Don't be stupid."

My cell buzzed.

"You got something?" Papa Joe said anxiously.

"Maybe, maybe not."

A raspy groan. "That all you wanna say?"

"How safe is this phone?"

"I got two dozen burn phones in my drawer. I toss this one as soon as we're done."

"Where are you?"

154

"My home office. I had the place debugged this morning."

"By who?"

"Don't worry about it. Whatta you got?"

"Know anything about the Coastal Grande casino in Biloxi?"

Silence. I figured I'd just hit pay-dirt.

"I own two casinos in Biloxi, *paisano*. I thought everyone knew that."

"The Coastal Grande one of them?"

A pause. "Why?"

The pause was short enough to tell me the right answer. Anything longer would have made things more complicated.

"Know anyone in Biloxi named Sid Raymer?"

Another pause. "Mebbe . . ."

"To answer your first question, I think I might be on to something."

"Tell me what you got."

"I can't say right now."

"Why not?"

"It's not how I work."

"Why do ya need to know about the Coastal Grande?"

"I'll get back to you." I hung up and pulled my binoculars from the glove box, focusing them on the six vehicles parked in front of the shopping mall across the street. An old maroon Ford pickup with NRA stickers covering the rear window sat in front of the tropical fish place next to the bookstore. A black SUV, a dirty white Honda Civic, and a filthy green Chevy S-10 pickup filled the spaces in front of the tee shirt/exotic pet store. Two vehicles obscured the entrance of the bookstore--an ancient dark-blue Camaro and a bright-red Mustang that looked like it had just come out of the showroom. The tag said *BERT O TOY*. Thank God for personalized tags.

"Tell me what happened when you went in the bookstore," I said to Mike.

"He was in his office with the door closed. I caught him at his desk, playing on his laptop. I think he was day-trading."

"Hmmm. . . ."

"What's that mean?"

"It means I think Berto has outgrown his hippie days and has ventured into what truly makes up Corporate America."

"I hope you're going to explain that."

"This guy has definitely turned to greed. And with greed comes betrayal."

"You got all that from his day-trading?"

"And from that fancy red Mustang, which ain't cheap."

"He *is* a businessman. And he *does* own a business."

"So?"

"He's bound to have money put away. He should be able to buy any car he wants."

"Maybe, but certain important things are practically shouting at me."

"I wish you'd tell me what they're shouting."

"I have this strong feeling Shields is one of Papa Joe's drivers. While you were inside, Neil called and told me Shields was arrested last month for doing coke in the men's room of the Coastal Grande Casino in Biloxi."

"So? What makes you think he's a driver?"

"Remember when I first met you?"

"What does that have to do with--"

"Just answer the question."

"We first met in the men's room at--"

"I mean when you first started helping me with that deadbeat dad case."

"Of course I remember."

"When you found out about Raguzzo's cocaine connection, you found out more than you realized."

"Go on . . ."

"He was there in the middle of the month. This goes back to our deadbeat dad case, when you found out Raguzzo's drivers do four weekly shipments a month."

"Is this enough to suspect the mob could be using him as a driver?"

"Not by itself, but I think it's kind of suspicious Shields was in the Coastal Grande, when there are dozens of other casinos in that same area."

"Why is that suspicious?"

"Raguzzo owns the Coastal Grande."

"I see . . ."

"To make things even more interesting, Shields was bailed out almost immediately after he was hauled in. Unless he's got connections in Biloxi we don't know about, someone was watching out for him and went to great lengths to make sure he didn't stay in jail very long."

"I finally see how you're putting all this together."

"Right now, it's still conjecture. I've got to catch him doing something if I want to find out what's really going on."

"Let me guess. You're waiting for him to leave the bookstore."

"Amazing how smart you've become just from hanging around with me."

"I know. This is really exciting and fascinating."

"You don't have to gush, you know."

"Sorry."

"We might have to be here a while." I checked my watch. "It's not even three. Shields might be here until five or six."

"On a Saturday?"

"You didn't happen to spot his hours on the front door, did you?"

"Sorry."

"No problem. We'll just wait until he comes out."

"Then what?"

"I haven't gotten any farther than that in my thinking."

"You probably need to think more, then. I'll leave you alone."

"Are you going somewhere again?"

"I need another recharge. I won't be far."

"Good. I tend to get into trouble when you're gone."

"That's why I always stay close." Then she faded away.

159

Chapter Thirteen

At ten minutes after three, Shields came out of the bookstore and got in the Mustang.

The unruly white hair stood out clearly even at a distance and in the shade of the awning. Apparently in a hurry, he backed out quickly, rushed over to the curb and shot right out, merging into the southbound flow.

I put the binoculars back in the glove box. I fired up the TransAm, crossed the lot and pulled up to the exit. A heavy knot of traffic chugged by, blocking my escape. I forced myself to wait. This wasn't the time to be impatient. My chance would come.

About two minutes later--which felt more like half an hour--the opportunity finally presented itself. I mashed down on the gas and quickly joined another slow-moving group to begin my pursuit.

The glittering red roof of the Mustang showed brightly about one block ahead. Shields stayed with the southbound flow until the intersection at West Michigan came up. He turned right, heading west.

I kept my distance and didn't mind when three vehicles cut in front of me. I wanted several cars separating us. I had to assume Shields knew about the TransAm. Since he'd told Beard and Blondie about me and had given them money to carjack me, he obviously knew the car I drove. This wasn't what bothered me. I cared much more about the person who'd told Shields what car I drove.

160

Traffic remained heavy. Saturday afternoon was great for shopping, restaurant-hopping, and trips to tourist attractions. Each filling station and eatery we passed proudly displayed a chaotic parking lot.

About fifteen minutes later, I coasted up to a knot of vehicles waiting impatiently at the intersection of Michigan and South Orange Blossom Trail. When the light changed, Shields made a left, and I kept in the southbound flow. The bumper-to-bumper traffic refused to thin, and I found myself fighting nausea as I passed the same porn shops for the second time in just a couple of hours.

"I see we're back in your favorite neighborhood." Mike had materialized beside me.

"It's my home away from home."

"Since you're back, you ought to use their facilities."

"I'd rather have a lobotomy with a dull ice pick."

By the time we passed 35th Street, the traffic had thinned out, making my tail job more difficult. I slowed down and kept the shiny red Stang in my sights, until it turned left, heading east on 39th Street.

Just before reaching the intersection, I pulled into the crowded filling station on the north side of the street, crossing the lot and inching past the pumps and the trimmed hedges at the turnoff. The bushes obscured my view at the corner, but I didn't proceed any further. I didn't want to run the risk of

Shields spotting the front of the TransAm sticking out if he checked his side mirror.

"Can you see what he's doing?" I asked Mike.

She began rising in her seat, until only her shapely calves and pumps showed. It was truly a strange sight. Just a few seconds later, she lowered herself until she was back in the seat. "Still heading east," she said.

"Damn, I wish I could do stuff like that."

"You'd have to die first."

"Good point." I pulled out, maintaining a slow, steady pace while keeping alert for emergency turnoffs.

About a mile later, the neighborhood became quietly residential, lined with trees, shrubbery, and palmettos. The Mustang slowed, turning right and easing up the short drive of a one-story block house with green shutters and a peaked roof. Large bushes spanned the length of the house. Palmettos grew tall and thick at each corner. A black Mercedes sat in front of a large storage building. Shields parked beside it.

I drove on by, noting the number *28* stenciled in gold on the right side of the black mailbox. There was no name. The property next to it sat secluded behind a long row of tall shrubbery. "Perfect setting for privacy."

"Want me to check it out?"

"If you don't mind. I'll try to find a place to ditch the car."

I went up to Wood Avenue and turned around, heading back toward the Trail. The building at the

162

corner looked like an apartment complex. I pulled into the large side lot, found a vacant space on the other side of a van, and parked. I took the .380 out of the console, grabbed my maroon windbreaker and shrugged into it. It was nearly eighty degrees, but I needed to conceal the gun, and my pants were too tight to permit me to get at it in a hurry. I dropped it in the inside pocket of the windbreaker and got out.

Mike met me as soon as I started toward the house.

"There are crates of stuff stacked on metal racks inside that storage building," she said.

"Any idea what the stuff is?"

"Bundles wrapped in brown paper and taped together."

"How big are the bundles?"

"About the size of two reams of typewriter paper. They were all the same, too."

"That narrows it down."

"I think the bundles are filled with drugs or money. Whatever it is, it's valuable."

"What makes you say that?"

"There's a large man inside the little office in the front of the building, and he's watching the property from a monitor."

"That *is* interesting."

"He's also wearing a gun."

***

The tall shrubbery fronting the side property hid me from view.

As I walked down the street, I kept looking for another way in. Unless I found a front entrance, I'd have to circle the block and work my way back in through the rear, from the woods. The guard would be watching every corner of the property. If there were cameras monitoring the woods, I might be able to spot them while keeping myself concealed by the trees and the underbrush.

I was interested only in the house. This property could be owned by local drug dealers to keep their shipments on ice until it was time to transport them. Shields had come here pretty quickly. I had to find out why.

"I've got to see what's going on in the house," Mike said, "before someone spots you and decides to take you somewhere and lock you in the trunk of your car."

"You had to bring that up again, didn't you?"

"Poor choice of words?"

"Maybe, but it actually sounds like a pretty good idea."

She smiled. "What do you want me to look for?"

"I need to know why Shields is here. I've got an idea what this place is, but I need to know for sure."

"It's where these mob guys keep their drugs, isn't it?"

"Since there's an armed guard and cameras, it could be. If this place belongs to Papa Joe, I think we're right-on about Shields being one of his drivers. If something else is going on, we might

164

have stumbled onto something useful. I'm getting strong vibes about this setup."

"If Shields is one of Raguzzo's drivers, why would he pay those two kids to kidnap you?"

"I intend to ask him as soon as I get him alone."

"I'll be right back," she said, and disappeared.

I kept walking. Less than a minute later, I heard the roar of two engines firing up. Even at this distance, I could tell one of them was the Mustang. I spun around and began walking back toward the house in question. I didn't get ten steps before I saw the Mustang backing out onto the street, then heading west, toward the Trail. The black Mercedes followed close behind.

Dammit. I'd obviously just missed something important going down.

I broke into a fast run. I had to get back to the TransAm and find out where they were going in such a hurry.

"No need to follow them." Mike reappeared on my left.

I stopped running. "What's happening?"

"They're going somewhere to dump the body. They mentioned using a dumpster behind one of the shopping plazas."

"Whose body?"

"Shields."

I gasped. "Shields is *dead*?"

"They wouldn't need to dump him if he was alive, would they?"

***

165

I didn't even try looking for the Mustang or the Mercedes as I drove north on the Trail. But I knew not to panic. Mike might have seen or heard something that could clear up some of this.

"What went on at the house?" I asked.

"There were two of them with Shields, and one was fixing drinks. One guy was sitting in a recliner while the other guy stood at the wet bar, fixing drinks. The guy at the bar hardly said anything. The other man was nasty to Shields, shouting and calling him names. He got up, grabbed the drinks, and handed a glass to Shields."

"Can you describe these two?"

"The one at the bar had brown hair. He was kind of thin, and around thirty. The other man was a few years older, tall and really well dressed. He had thick wavy black hair and obviously spent a lot of money on it. His clothes, too. He wore a silk white shirt and black pants, and his shoes were black patent leather and looked imported."

"No accents?"

"The well-dressed guy sounded Spanish."

"How could you tell?"

"I can usually tell when someone's Spanish, even if they don't have an accent. Certain words give them away."

I knew what she meant. Living in Florida most of my life had made it easy to distinguish accents. "Tell me about the argument."

"Shields kept saying it wasn't his fault. He said you can't tell what someone's gonna do, especially if they've never done that kind of work before.

Then he asked them to give him another chance. He reminded them how long he'd been with them. Then the black-haired guy reminded him how stupid he was to get nailed by the cops in the middle of a job. Shields said he was framed for that. Someone wanted him out of the way so they could take his job. That was how the casino cops found out about him. Guys went into the john to snort up all the time. It was no big deal. Then he finished his drink and told them he'd make sure he got the job done right this time."

"Then what?"

Mike shrugged. "He just keeled over and collapsed."

"Just like that?"

"It was really sudden."

"They spiked his drink."

"I guess they decided not to give him another chance."

"Think you can remember these two if you see them again?"

"Definitely."

***

I pulled into the crowded McDonald's and went over to a shaded space on the other side of the building, near some trees and trimmed hedges.

It was nearly four o'clock, and my gut had been making horrible sounds in protest. It didn't appreciate being empty for so long and was giving me hell. I promised it I'd take care of business after I made an important call. It eased up for a moment,

167

but I could tell the reprieve would be only temporary.

"What the hell is it this time?" As always, Sonny Bergman sounded like I'd interrupted him in the middle of a major bowel movement. "What is this? The tenth time you called today? I'm trying to run a business!"

"It's only my second call, Sonny, and I wouldn't bother you if I didn't have to."

"I know, I know. Gimme two minutes." Then he hung up.

"They're not very nice, are they?" Mike asked.

"Why do you think I never have them over for poker and beer?"

"Because you don't play poker?"

"That's one good reason."

"And because you don't want them in your apartment?"

"That's another good one."

My cell buzzed. It was Papa Joe.

"How's this business going?" He sounded much calmer than before. He'd obviously convinced himself I knew what I was doing and would actually solve this case for him. Or maybe he'd just taken some meds.

"Know anything about a place on 39th Street?"

Silence. I didn't know if I'd just hit another nerve. It would have helped if I'd seen his expression. Papa Joe was a master at hiding things. He had a sixth sense about when to talk, when to keep quiet and when to lie. Right now he might be trying to decide what to tell me. Or maybe he just couldn't remember.

"It don't ring no bells. Why?"

He didn't sound like he was hiding anything, but I couldn't be sure. Being a mob boss--as well as a shrewd businessman--came with certain requirements. Keeping your hand from being seen was quite possibly one of the most important.

"You don't own any property in that area?"

"I like Disney property. Better land, and you never lose your investment. Plus, you no have to worry about the wrong people coming in and bringing down the values."

"Sure you don't know what I'm talking about?"

"Like I said, it don't ring no bells. What's this got to do with me and my business?"

"It might have something to do with one of your competitors, and whoever ordered that hit on me."

More silence. Papa Joe wasn't his usual abrasive self, indicating that he was trying to assess what I was asking him. If he was hiding anything, he'd be much more defensive and abrupt.

I'd saved the next part for last, hoping for a sharper reaction. "I have to talk to someone who works in Biloxi."

Silence.

I had a hunch he was going to be slippery. I'd hoped he'd confide in me more but wasn't surprised to hear the heavy pause on the line. I had to remind myself of the position he was in. He'd spent years putting up that barrier. It had saved his life a number of times and also helped him build his empire. I couldn't expect him to drop it so easily.

I had to approach this tactfully, or I'd upset everything. "Let me put it another way. I need to talk to someone handling your out-of-state business dealings."

"My company has many different investments, *paisano*. I own restaurants, some of them in Miami and Tampa. I own strip clubs, and some are in Tampa as well as here. I even own a golf course."

"I'm interested only in your Biloxi dealings."

"I take it we're talking about my two casinos."

"I guess so."

"What about them?"

"Do the employees handle everything up there?"

"One of my investment outfits manages their payroll."

This "being tactful" shtick was getting on my last nerve, but I had to do it this way. I couldn't let him know I'd found out about his out-of-state operation two years ago. He'd freak. He might even think I was one of the people going against him.

"How do you do that? Online transfers?"

"I'm too damn old for that bullshit. Sleazeballs hack in and steal account information and transfer the funds into dummies they got set up in different countries. You go in there one day to move your money around and end up staring at all those zeroes and wondering where your fucking accounts ran off to."

"So you personally move the money?"

"It's the safest way."

I sighed. This was taking entirely too long, but there was no other way. On the flip side, I was almost there. "You use UPS?"

"What, stick the money in a box and hand it over to some fool kid in brown shorts making thirty K a year? You kidding or what?"

"I guess you use drivers . . ."

"No other way of doing it."

I felt like celebrating. "Any way I could talk to one of them?"

"If I arrange it."

"I'd appreciate it if you could set up a meeting with one of your drivers."

"That's Giorgio. He manages my drivers, schedules the trips and makes sure the money's ready to go. He keeps my boys on a monthly schedule."

"Then he'd know who's gonna make the next trip as well as who made the last trip?"

"I just told you, he arranges everything."

"What's Giorgio look like?"

"Why you need to know?"

"People have already tried to kill me twice-- remember?" I decided not to tell him about my colorful excursion through Orlando's seedy side with Beard and Blondie. I didn't want to sour this pleasant conversation.

"Giorgio's around thirty-five. About your height, maybe a little taller, and big boned. Likes his pasta. Black hair, black eyes. Does what he's told. He'll talk to you if I tell him to."

"You trust him?"

"He's a good man."

"That doesn't answer my question."

A deep sigh. "Yeah. I trust Giorgio--I'm godfather for two of his boys. Good enough?"

"Have you forgotten why you hired me?"

"Deacon, do what you gotta do, okay?"

"I just don't want you to be surprised what I dig up."

"I'll live with it, *capire*?"

"I'm about fifteen minutes from Vesper's. Will this Giorgio be at the club? Or should I head on over to the airport and get tickets for the Cayman Islands? Or maybe Switzerland?"

"He's got an office at the club, hotshot. He'll be there right now."

Chapter Fourteen

At ten minutes after four, Vesper's was experiencing a lull.

Club business usually thinned out for about an hour during the dinner hour, starting back up at five-thirty and returning to full capacity by six.

After a cheeseburger, fries and a vanilla shake, I felt comfortably full, and eager to talk with Giorgio. I parked in a spot two rows down from the front, and Mike and I went up the paved drive leading to the front entrance, where two massive slabs of flesh guarded the huge double doors.

"These aren't the same two I saw last time we came," Mike said.

"How can you tell?"

"These two are bigger."

"How can you tell?"

"Good point."

Both glandular cases regarded me curiously as I paid the cover. I wanted to think they were impressed by the way I carried myself, but I knew better. They were probably wondering who I'd just been talking to. Introducing them to Mike would be interesting, but it might also get me tossed to the curb. I couldn't talk to Giorgio if I was sitting by the curb, swollen and bleeding.

Mike and I went inside, where the smoky blue lighting in the large, well-decorated room hovered like a lazy cloud above the activity. Scantily clad waitresses, their tanned, sweat-stained flesh gleaming, avoided probing hands as they slipped quickly through wandering clots of horny men.

"I'm glad I'm dead," Mike said as we made our way toward the archway marked *OFFICES*.

"Why's that?"

"If I was alive, my butt would be sore from all the slaps and pinching I see going on."

"Your butt is high-class," I said. "It deserves to be slapped and pinched."

The red-headed waitress passing us shot me an icy glare.

"Thanks very much," Mike said, "and please stop insulting the waitresses."

"It was a compliment. And I was talking to *you*."

"You'd better go tell her."

"She'll think I'm crazy--as well as a pervert."

"But at least you'll feel better, knowing you tried doing the right thing."

We went through the archway, and a broad-shouldered guy in a tight suit appeared in the hall, approaching me. "Ya lost?"

"Not this time."

He pointed toward the main room. "The booze and girls are back there, where ya just came."

"I need to talk to Giorgio."

"Who are ya?"

"Tell him Deacon."

"Deacon?"

"Good memory. He knows I'm here to see him."

174

The man looked doubtful. He also looked suspicious. He was probably trying to decide if he should search me, pick me up and carry me outside, or just say hell with it and let me see Giorgio.

"If you don't believe me, just tell Sonny you won't let Deacon talk to Giorgio. I'd like to stick around to see how long it takes before you're tossed out into the street."

He must have believed me; he instantly straightened and blinked out of his dark fugue of doubt. "Stay put." He marched briskly down the hall and knocked on the door at the far end. He opened it and disappeared inside. Five seconds later, he came back out into the hall and gestured for me.

Mike and I went down the hall toward him, until we came to the door marked *G. Matteo, Investments Manager*. Our reluctant escort opened the door. Mike and I went in, and he closed the door softly behind us.

The man behind the desk stood and extended a hand. He fit Papa Joe's description closely enough to convince me this was the man we'd talked about. About six feet tall, he weighed in at around two-forty and looked like he belonged in the cast of *The Sopranos*. His curly black hair, large dark eyes and olive complexion screamed Sicilian.

"Mr. Deacon?" he asked in a soft, low-pitched voice.

"That's me," I said. The handshake was firm, dry, and brief. I was surprised by the way he'd addressed me. I usually got Deacon, *Stronzone*, Slick, Jack, Man, Mac, Dude, or just plain Asshole.

I wanted to thank him but knew better than assume anything with this bunch. The fact that he was polite and soft-spoken didn't mean he wasn't the one who'd sent two hit men after me.

People who are polite and order contract hits tend to get on my nerves.

"Please. Have a seat."

I sat and he returned to his seat as well.

"What Did Papa Joe say about me?"

"He told me to cooperate with you and not give you any shit--to use his language."

So far, so good. I didn't sense any animosity or resistance. "He say why?"

"Only that you were working for him in an investigative capacity."

I nodded.

Mike drifted over to the bookcase behind Matteo and browsed some of the titles. "He must love Alberto Moravia." She turned. "Ever heard of him?"

"Yeah."

"Pardon me?" Matteo asked.

"This is an investigation. You like Moravia?"

"He apparently loves him," Mike said. "There are twenty titles here."

Matteo raised his thick black brows and turned to where Mike was standing. He turned back to me; he was squinting. "You can *see* the books from there?"

I shrugged.

"They're paperbacks. The titles are, well, small."

176

"Good eyesight."

"Obviously--especially for a man, well"--he grinned sheepishly--"no longer in his teens."

"Uh-oh." Mike tiptoed away from the bookcase.

"I take after my father," I said flatly. "He could sit in the living room and read his meds even when the bottle was out in the kitchen." I needed to get a facelift--or shoot this jerk when the case was over. I decided against the facelift--a bullet would be cheaper.

Noticing my discomfort, Matteo shifted in his seat. "Yes. I love the man's writing." Changing the subject seemed a dandy idea. "*Two Women* has always been a personal favorite. How 'bout you?"

"Haven't checked him out, actually. Maybe next year, when I'm sitting in the retirement home with nothing else to do."

Matteo squirmed a little more, making me feel better. "Can you, um, tell me anything more about any of . . . of why you're here?"

"Not really. It's an ongoing investigation."

"I see. . ." He sat forward and rested his elbows on the desk top. He seemed to have recovered-- which *didn't* make me feel better. I expected his embarrassment to last longer than five seconds. However, these characters weren't normal. They had no trouble ordering hits on their way to church for their daughter's baptism, or Easter services.

"Papa Joe tells me you handle his drivers."

"We have a pool of six. We use two each week."

"Do you have someone named Shields on your payroll?"

"Albert? Yes. He's been with us a couple of years."

"Can you tell me the last time he drove to Biloxi?"

Matteo opened his large green hardbound logbook and scanned a column with a thick index finger. It only took him five seconds. "Last week."

"Before that?"

He consulted the logbook again. "Two weeks before."

"That would have been the middle of the month?"

"Correct."

"And when is he due to drive again?"

"Next week. Each driver makes a trip every two or three weeks, depending on who's available."

"What do they do when they're not driving?"

"Warehouse work, mostly. They'll take the liquor shipments off the trucks and cart them in by forklift to the warehouse, where they're stored. It keeps them busy."

"Have you had any trouble with Shields?"

"Trouble?"

"Disciplinary."

He shook his head. "Arthur's a model employee. Anyway, he's only part-time. He's not here very much."

"Part-time?"

"He's strictly a driver. We don't want him doing any hard physical work--which is okay with

178

him, since he's more than twenty years older than the others. He owns and runs a bookstore in town, so he stays busy when he's not driving for us. Anyway, disciplinary stuff doesn't happen too much in our business. You cause trouble, you're out." He shrugged.

"Out?"

"Fired. Papa Joe hates problems."

"I can't imagine Sonny putting up with them, either."

Matteo smiled. "You must know Sonny."

"Sufficiently."

"Then you know why he's been running the club for so long."

"He's tough."

"You have to be in this business. Is there anything else I can help you with, Mr. Deacon?"

"You said each driver makes his trip once every two or three weeks. Are the same two always grouped together?"

"Unless something comes up, or someone calls in. All six drivers know one another, so it really doesn't matter, since they all get along."

"Does Shields have anyone in particular he pals around with?"

"Paul Givens is another of our drivers. He and Shields are buddies. They usually make their trips together as well."

"Paul Givens?"

"Both men have been with us the same amount of time. Givens is much younger than Shields and took his classes at UCF. Did I tell you Shields teaches college in the summer?"

"You didn't mention that."

"Well, they're pretty close. Givens even rents a bedroom in Shields' apartment. They've been living together several years."

"Can you describe Givens?"

"He's around thirty, with brown hair and brown eyes. He's thinning a little on top, and he's about five-ten and doesn't weigh much more than one-fifty or so."

"Where's this apartment?"

Matteo hesitated.

"You probably don't want to give out such personal information, but Papa Joe would approve. I have his authorization. And I promise I'll be discreet."

"In that case. . ." Matteo consulted his Rolodex. "On Palmetto, just off West Jefferson. Palmetto Arms Apartments, Room Seventeen A."

"That should do it."

"Is that all you need?"

"Pretty much."

Matteo got up and extended his hand again.

I thanked him and left his office.

"He was nice," Mike said.

"A real peach."

"Was it his comment about your excellent eyesight that has you upset?"

"It didn't exactly make me want to invite him over to my place for beer and pizza, if that's what you mean."

"He was right, though. No one's eyes are that good. I'll bet he couldn't even read them from there, and he's younger than you."

"If you're trying to help, you need to start over."

"Actually, I thought he was much more of a gentleman than those other people you have to deal with."

"Maybe . . ."

"But you still don't like him, do you?"

"I'll like him if I find out he wasn't involved in that hit on me."

Chapter Fifteen

We got back on the Trail and went north, toward the downtown area.

Even though it was Saturday and there was no rush hour, traffic remained chaotic. Tourists seem to have a particular talent for making the roads worse than they should be.

"We're going to see that Paul Givens guy, aren't we?" Mike asked.

"You really do pay attention," I said.

"I have to. When I don't, you get beat up or knocked unconscious."

It was thoughtful of her to bring that up. It did a lot for my self-image. "I'm so glad you've got such confidence in me."

"I respect you, too."

"I'll bet."

"Why the skeptical look?"

"Maybe that's because I'm, well, skeptical."

"You shouldn't be. You're doing a fine job of solving this on your own."

"Not *all* on my own . . ."

"Oh, I just step in occasionally to do things you can't possibly do yourself."

"You're making me sound incompetent and stupid."

"Can you walk through walls?"

"You know I can't."

"Turn invisible?"

"Of course not."

"Walk into a bad guy's office without him knowing you're there?"

I sighed.

"Satisfied?"

"When you put it that way. . ." It still made me feel incompetent and stupid.

It was nearly five-thirty when I reached Palmetto and parked in the large open lot between buildings.

A large yellow block structure, Palmetto Arms sat sandwiched between other apartment complexes and a massive parking garage. Its underground parking garage was accessible through the front and also from the stairs at the ground entrance. Long rows of balcony terraces spanned the length of the building.

Judging by the address Giorgio Matteo had provided, Shields' apartment sat on the first floor. This suited me fine. I hated heights and didn't want to risk being tossed from a balcony window. I'd escaped death three times in the last twenty-four hours and didn't want to tempt fate.

The lobby was sparsely decorated with half a dozen plastic plants, a well-worn plaid couch and a couple of chairs that looked like they'd been taken from a cheap motel. The elevators faced the front. On their left, a narrow hall led to the ground floor apartments.

Mike and I went down the dimly lit carpeted hall, which smelled of cigarettes, bleach, and someone's cheap aftershave. A crumpled cigarette wrapper and shards of broken glass glittering in the worn green carpet told me their housekeeper had neglected her rounds.

17A sat three doors down from the end of the corridor. *Shields/Givens*, printed neatly in ink on a small white card inserted in the metal slot, showed above the glass peephole.

"Want me to go inside?" Mike asked.

I nodded.

She vanished through the door.

When she reappeared just ten seconds later, her face, which usually glowed, had a reddish tinge to it.

"What's happening in there?" I whispered.

"They're . . . having sex. Well, *he* is."

"Who's they? And whaddya mean, he is?"

"The Givens guy. There's a woman in there with him, and she's . . . well, she's . . . going down . . . on him."

I couldn't stop the grin that quickly covered my face.

Mike wasn't amused. "I wasn't exactly ready for that, you know."

I had to force myself from coming up with my usual quips. Mike was uncomfortable. I didn't want her to disappear. "I understand. That *is* shocking and obscene."

Her features remained taut. "Somehow you don't sound upset enough."

I shrugged. "I'm on a job. I've got to set aside all my personal prejudices and force myself to remain cold and objective."

"You don't look cold and objective."

"How do I look?"

184

"Anyone can tell you're holding back a huge belly laugh."

"I would never laugh when you're so uncomfortable."

"Thank you for that." But her cold stare told me she didn't believe me.

"So . . . now that we both know how we stand on certain issues, what else did you find out--other than Mister Givens has been fortunate enough to find a lady who obviously appreciates the benefits of a good facial?"

She groaned. "Can you *please* rephrase that?"

"Okay, okay. What else did you find out?"

"He's one of the two men I saw at the place on 39th Street."

"You mean--"

"He was the one who mixed Albert Shields' drink."

***

While Mike slipped inside the apartment again, I knocked on the door.

My plan was simple. I came to ask to see Shields about a rare book I'd been looking for. Since Givens couldn't possibly know that I was aware of his involvement in the murder of his roommate, he shouldn't be on his guard. However, any hostility or fear on his part would convince me he knew who I was. This would be clear evidence that he was directly involved in this mess.

In any case, I was taking a big risk. Givens might come to the door with a gun in his hand. Even so, I had to take the risk. There were too many pieces missing in this puzzle. I couldn't solve anything unless I forced someone's hand.

The door opened. It was the babe.

Up close, she was a feast for the eyes. I tried my best not to salivate, but I knew right off that I was fighting a losing battle.

Testosterone can be a man's worst enemy at a time like this.

At least five-eleven in her bare feet, she wore loose-fitting red shorts and a sleeveless yellow blouse opened at the neck to reveal a tatt covering the top of her left breast. She wasn't wearing a bra, but her breasts stuck straight out and could probably serve as a couple of handy tie racks. I forced myself from asking her to remove her blouse so I could see the tatt better. And also to decide once and for all if those babies were natural, or the triumph of some top-rate plastics manufacturer. That would be rude. I had to maintain my dignity. Standing so close to a woman who'd just given head to a man two minutes earlier was difficult.

"Want somethin'?" She sounded disinterested but kept looking me up and down. Mostly down. Needless to say, it made me even more uncomfortable. Her long, platinum-blond hair slid provocatively down her shoulders. Her long-lashed green eyes, pouty lips, and long shapely legs, as well as those bodacious jugs, told me she was a stripper. With her looks, she could easily be one of Papa Joe's top-rated girls.

"I came to see Berto."

She stiffened. Her eyes grew.

She obviously knew Shields was dead. She turned away. I saw no less than eight silver studs starting at the top of her ear and trailing all the way down to the small pink lobe. There was also a silver stud at the left corner of her mouth, and a barbed wire tatt encircling her left bicep.

I considered it a crime, disfiguring such perfect flesh.

"Berto told me to see him about a book I've been trying to find."

Recovering, she took a breath, tilted her head, and squinted at me. "Book?" Her expression made me wonder if she had any idea what I was talking about.

"It comes with a cover and a title, and a whole bunch of pages inside. Some folks use them for doorstops while others actually read the words on the pages--"

"I know what a book is," she said sourly. A heavy platinum ringlet slid down her front, covering the tatt. I decided it would be much healthier for me not to nudge it away. "Berto . . . he ain't in."

"That's funny."

"Funny?"

"He told me to come see him today or tomorrow."

"Well, he ain't in."

"When do you expect him back?"

She turned away again. I suspected she wanted Givens to come over and help her out.

"Tomorrow, maybe? Any time's good for me."

Mike suddenly reappeared beside me. "He just got off the phone."

"I dunno when he'll be back," the babe said. "He don't tell me where he's goin'. We ain't . . . close."

"Isn't this his apartment? His name's on the door."

"My boyfriend lives here, too. I'm . . . seein' him."

Seeing *him? Is* that *what they're calling that nowadays?*

Mike moved closer to me. "He told whoever he called that you're here, and that they could pick you up outside when you leave."

That was it, then. Givens had just screwed himself, big-time.

"Could I talk to your boyfriend?" I asked the babe. "Maybe he knows where—"

"Berto never tells me nothing." Givens appeared behind the babe, peering around her. I couldn't see his left side.

"He's got a gun," Mike said.

I'd figured as much. Since he'd already called about me, he wouldn't want to use the gun. Besides, the babe might get hit. He probably intended to scare me with it if I tried to enter the apartment. "He didn't by any chance tell you one of his customers--"

"He don't tell me *nothin'*, Mister. You deaf or somethin'?"

"I've been accused of that once or twice, usually by my mother. My ex-wife noticed it, too. That's not why she divorced me, though."

"Huh?" The babe looked confused.

"Just a little levity. Listen . . . if I leave my number, would you tell Berto--"

"I look like a fucking *secretary* to you?" Givens had the look of someone about to explode. It told me he clearly had sexual issues.

I shrugged and gave him the once-over. "Maybe if you shaved a little closer? Took hormone injections? Wore the right dress?"

The babe covered her smile with her left hand, which showed a tatt of a tiny blue star near the middle knuckle.

"Fuck you!" Givens yanked her inside and slammed the door in my face.

"How about if I give you my card?" I asked the door.

"*Fuck off!*"

"I'd give you my office number, but I'm having the walls repainted and I can't go in there for at least a week. Fumes, you know. They make me high, and I tend to do stupid things when I'm--"

"I'll call the cops if you don't get the fuck *outa* here!"

I turned away from the door. "Is he looking out the peephole?" I whispered to Mike.

"The girl's doing it."

"What's *he* doing?"

"Making another call."

"To who?"

She disappeared. When she came back, she said, "He asked what's taking them so long. They told him they ran into some snag on Colonial. They're about two minutes from East Jefferson, and he should try and stall you until they get here."

The door opened behind me as soon as I started walking down the hall.

"C'mon back, Mister," the babe said. "Wanna drink?"

"No, thanks." I didn't miss a step.

"I make good drinks!" She sounded urgent.

"I'll bet you do."

"We can talk, too. About . . . books?"

I turned around. "Isn't that kind of risky? Talking about books? With your boyfriend there? He'll feel, well, neglected. Maybe even stupid, too."

"He's . . . in the shower now. Lemme fix ya a drink."

"Maybe another time." I reached the end of the hall and cut around the corner, out through the lobby, sprinting back to the TransAm. "Still there?" I asked the open air.

"Still here." Mike was right behind me.

"At least we know which way they're coming. Even so, this'll be close."

I fired up the TransAm, tore out of the lot and shot north, up Palmetto, barely pausing at the *STOP* sign on West Robinson. I turned left, pulling into the vacant bank parking lot not far beyond the intersection. I found a secluded spot toward the back, behind some trimmed shrubbery, and parked the car.

190

"Now what?" Mike asked.

"We wait."

"For what?"

"For me to feel safe."

"And then?"

"I walk back to Givens' apartment and question him properly."

"Properly?"

"This time I'm bringing my gun."

***

While we waited, I called the DMV and got Veronica Seals, whom I'd known for a couple of years. Ronnie was an okay lady and had never minded doing me a favor.

"What can I do ya for, baby?" she said in her soft, low-pitched tone. Veronica looked nothing like her name or her voice. Around fifty or so, she stood five-two, tipped the scales at around one-eighty, and wore thick, large-rimmed glasses over her tiny, cornflower-blue eyes. Her curly red hair looked like a rusty Brillo pad sitting on a baseball. She smoked a lot, coughed, and cleared her throat constantly.

"The last lady who asked me that got me into serious trouble, Ronnie."

She cleared her throat. "It was prob'ly your own damned fault."

"I gotta do something to get noticed. My good looks don't seem to be enough these days."

"We ladies don't go for looks these days. Give us cash. We'll follow you anywhere."

"I'm a detective. I don't like being followed."

"'Nuff said. So whaddya need?"

"A make on someone giving me a rough time."

She let out a loud cackle, coughing wetly toward the end. "I don't have that kinda time, baby. Narrow it down a smidge."

"The name's Paul Givens. He's around thirty. Brown hair and eyes. He should have an Orlando address. He lives at the Palmetto Arms."

She coughed. "Gimme a minute."

A black Audi drove west on Jefferson, moving slowly in the right-hand lane. Since my view was obscured by the bushes, I only saw it a moment before it disappeared behind the bank. The dark-haired passenger had his head stuck out of the window. I saw the shape of someone else in the back seat.

"Is that them?" Mike asked.

"Probably."

"Probably what?" Veronica asked.

"Just talking to myself."

Another cackle. "Haven't changed much, have ya?"

"What fun would that be?"

"Here we go. Paul Givens. Age thirty-one. Drives a silver Mustang. This year's model. Need the tag number?"

"If you don't mind. . ."

"How's this for helping you out? P-A-U-L-S-R-I-D-E-1."

"Ronnie, one of these days, you and I are gonna--"

"I know, I know. I hear that every time I do ya a favor. Now do me one."

"Anything."

"Send cash."

"Just as soon as I get some."

"Heard that before, too," she said, and coughed wetly.

***

During the next hour, the Audi had circled the block twice more. After that, it was too dark to see anything.

I sat alone in the TransAm while Mike left for another recharge. When I thought the trio of henchmen had grown tired of their hunt, I stuck the .380 in the pocket of my windbreaker, opened the door and got out.

My heart raced as I hurried back down Palmetto. It was after seven, and the roads hummed with Saturday night traffic. I stayed a good distance from the curb, walking on the grass and keeping as far away from headlights as possible.

Fifteen minutes later, I reached Palmetto Arms, crossed the parking lot I'd used earlier and went down the metal staircase that led to the underground garage.

Although the garage was more than half-filled and many of the vehicles I saw were silver, gray, or white, I spotted it almost immediately. A silver Mustang stands out, its sleek shape very distinctive. I found it sitting just three rows down from the elevators, sandwiched between a green Saturn and a tan Toyota. The tag, *PAULSRIDE1*, made things ridiculously simple.

No one else was in the garage. Regardless of what people think, it isn't easy to sneak up on someone in a parking garage. The clicking of heels, the shuffling of papers, the roar of an engine firing up--even someone coughing, clearing their throat or lighting a cigarette--all echo, and carry easily. To grab someone, you've literally got to find the victim's vehicle and hide behind the nearest pillar or the vehicle next to it. It also helps if you're wearing tennis shoes, donning a mask, and have a chloroform packet out and ready.

The *ding*! of the elevator startled me. I ducked behind the Mustang. The red button above the car registered its brief descent from the ground floor.

The doors opened. Two men in dark clothes got out. Heels clicking almost in unison, they went down the aisle, away from me. Seconds later, I heard the thump of two doors slamming shut and the firing up of an engine. The loud moan of a vehicle backing up resonated off the concrete walls, and a light cloud of exhaust smoke drifted lazily by, irritating my nostrils. After the shifting of gears, the vehicle roared down the aisle past me. It was the black Audi.

In the ensuing silence, I began breathing normally again. I squatted between vehicles and let the air out of the Mustang's left rear tire. Then duck-walked up to the front tire and let the air out of it as well. When Givens came outside, he'd know he wouldn't be going anywhere for a while.

It was an expensive, beautiful car, much like Shields' red model. The fact that both had bought similar cars at basically the same time made it obvious that they'd hit a bonanza. Working for Papa Joe's opposition might have proven the perfect gig.

"This is very mean of you." Mike appeared beside me, shaking her head at my handiwork. "And nasty. And very juvenile."

"Your point?"

She looked confused. "This can't be another envy thing, can it? Like the silver Lexus?"

"I don't want Givens running away before I can question him."

"This was all you could come up with?"

"Shooting him in the leg would be a tad harsh. People are hard to question when they're in great pain, and bleeding profusely."

"I guess you have a point."

"Am I forgiven, then?"

"There's nothing to forgive, silly."

"I feel like there should be. Since you're yelling at me . . ."

"I *never* yell at you. I'm merely speaking my mind. I don't want you lowering yourself to the level of the thugs you're dealing with."

"Sometimes I have to. By the way, those three goons just left."

"I know. I passed them when I came in."

"They obviously talked to Givens. I just hope they didn't kill the poor bastard."

"Why would they?"

"For letting me slip away. For getting them here late. Because it's Saturday. Who knows?"

"If he's dead, you can't question him."

195

"I sort of figured that out on my own."

"Really?"

"My brain has been known to work even when you're not around."

"I'm *so* glad."

Chapter Sixteen

Before we reached the hall, I quietly told Mike my plan. "Here's the scenario. When I knock on the door--"

"Where will I be?"

"Right beside me."

"Good idea. I think you're gonna need me to be close."

"So do I. Anyway--"

"Please hurry. We don't have much time, and I don't want to forget anything and screw up your plan."

I sighed. "I'm trying to, but you keep interrupting me."

"Sorry."

"Anyway, after I knock, I'll move over to the side so I'm out of range of the peephole. You slip through the wall and see what they're doing. As soon as one of them unlocks the door and gets ready to crack it open, give me a signal."

"What kind of a signal?"

"Anything."

"How about a wave?"

"That's fine."

"Or would you like a wink instead?"

She was acting silly again. I told myself this was okay. It was Mike, so it was okay. "Anything you do will be just fine. Just so I know when to move."

"Sounds simple enough."

"One other thing. If he's got a gun, tell me that, too."

"You want a signal for that?"

"Okay, sure."

"How about if I just say, "gun"?"

"That'll work, too."

"Got it."

"You've recharged, right?"

"Why do you ask?"

"I can't have you disappearing during this. There are two of them in there, and one's a babe."

"So what?"

"She's hot. Good-looking. With extremely large breasticles. And she's half-naked."

"What difference does that make?"

"You're not serious."

"I guess I wasn't thinking, was I?"

I touched my .380, just to make sure it was still inside my jacket and hadn't somehow slipped through a hole in the fabric and disappeared. That was silly, but I tend to think strange things in dangerous situations. I tiptoed the last couple of yards, until I reached Room 17A. I banged on it three times and quickly moved off to the side, waiting tensely, my back against the wall and my left hand inside my jacket, gripping the butt of the .380.

Mike's image dissolved into the wall.

Silence.

Ten seconds later, her image reappeared. "Gun," she said. I nodded, and she said, "Knock again."

198

I knocked and immediately moved away.

Seconds later, the sound of a deadbolt clicked heavily.

Mike reappeared. She held up a hand and quickly lowered it.

I rushed up to the door and forced it wide-open with my shoulder. The door slammed into something, driving a loud grunt from whoever was inside. My gun out, I leaped inside and grabbed the edge of the door with my right hand, slamming it shut and locking it.

Paul Givens rolled around on the carpet, clutching his forehead. Blood gushed from his mouth and nose. A severe gash just below his left eye had already turned blue. I didn't think I'd caused that.

The blonde stood in the hall about ten feet away, both hands covering her mouth. Her right eye looked like someone had belted her. She wore a pair of pink transparent panties with red lace and a pair of shiny red open-toed spikes. Nothing else. The spikes made her six-two or -three, easy.

As soon as my eyes finally wandered down to the red spikes, I noticed the gun lying on the carpet in front of her, just three feet from where Givens lay.

"*Fuck*! Ya fucking *brained* me!" He held his forehead with his right hand.

"Someone like you needs all the help he can get." I bent and grabbed the gun. It was a .22 revolver with a four-inch barrel and a plastic grip. A Saturday night special. This didn't make sense.

Anyone who could afford a prime ride like that silver Stang downstairs would have a decent gun.

"Man . . . who the fuck *are* ya?"

"I'm offended. You honestly don't know?"

He stayed on his back, massaging his forehead with one hand and holding his nose with the other. "How the fuck am I s'posed to know that?"

"What about those three glandular cases you sent after me?"

He gawked at me between his hands. "Huh?"

"You know what I'm talking about. Those three wet boys in that black Audi who came here just as soon as I left. You want to tell me you didn't know about them?"

"Man, I don't know what the fuck you're *talkin'* about!"

The blonde continued trembling, her hands still covering her mouth. Her silicone specials were exposed, and I could clearly see the tatt over her left tit. It was some sort of artsy-fartsy pink leaf design spilling down her cleavage in a cascade of petals, gathering around her navel in a garland of roses. She also had tatts of names on her thighs, another barbed wire tatt encircling her right upper arm, and a rose petal on each hip.

Damn, she was distracting. If I hadn't been so concerned with Givens, I would have spent more time examining her body art. I hoped she wouldn't do anything that would make me have to tie her up. Tying up a naked, six-foot woman with big boobs is probably the most distracting thing a man could ever do.

I motioned with both guns. "C'mon over here and sit down," I told her. "And take off those pumps." I figured she'd be less distracting in her bare feet.

She was either frightened or in shock; she raised her arms instead. I noticed a rose petal in her right armpit and found myself struggling to focus again.

"Try harder." Mike was frowning beside me. "You're being *such* a guy again."

I nodded. "Listen, sweetie. And pay attention. Lower your arms, okay?"

Still trembling, she lowered them.

"Good. Now . . . walk over there and sit down on the couch."

She nearly tripped on one of her spikes but managed to lower that perfect butt onto the cushion without killing herself or breaking an ankle.

"Now take off those damned spikes."

She watched me curiously as she pulled one off, then the other. She looked confused. "I thought guys liked spikes."

"Love 'em. I've even dreamed about them on cold, wintry nights. A pair like those would probably bring me back from the dead. But right now, I need to focus on more important stuff."

"That was tacky," Mike said. "Even for you."

"It's the truth," I told her.

"That's what I was afraid of," she said.

"Huh?" the blonde asked, blinking.

"Man . . . my fuckin' head feels like *shit*!" Givens clutched his forehead.

"Want me to get you a cold washcloth?" I asked.

He nodded. "That'd be nice."

"I'll bet you'd like me to fix you a drink, too."

Givens squinted up at me. Even a clueless idiot like him could sense sarcasm.

"Tell you what. If you're a good boy, maybe this fine lady here will get you a washcloth and even a strong drink. After I leave, of course."

Givens remained squinting. "Whaddya want? Who the fuck *are* ya? Why'd you break into my place?"

"So many questions, so little time."

The blonde suddenly remembered she was naked. She looked down at herself, then at me. She gasped, covering her breasts with her arms.

"You don't have to do that, you know," I said. "I've seen breasts before. Not that those aren't really nice, but . . ."

"We really need to have a serious talk one of these days." Mike glared at me.

The blonde lowered her arms an inch. She glanced at Givens, then me. Sighing, she raised them again.

I wanted to shoot Givens for making her do that.

"Get up," I told him. "Go over to the couch and sit down beside your girlfriend. We need to talk."

"Man--"

"You heard me."

"But--"

"Shut up and do it." I pulled back the hammer of the revolver.

The blonde cringed. I felt badly for scaring her, but since I didn't know how involved she was, I had to suspect them both. For all I knew, it was her idea to send Blondie and Beard after me. That was a stretch, but I couldn't rule it out.

Givens rolled over, pushed himself up and crawled over to the couch. Using the cushion for leverage, he pulled himself up, slid his ass onto it and collapsed. In addition to the gash just above his left cheekbone and the bloody lip, his forehead gleamed red. The thugs in the black Audi had given him a rough evening.

An armchair faced the couch. I went over and sat down. "Everyone comfy?"

Givens moaned. The blonde continued staring at the guns in my hands.

I cracked open the revolver, tilted it back and let the six small brass cartridges spill into my lap. I pocketed them, snapped the gun shut and let it rest on my left thigh. "Better?"

She blinked. "Almost."

"Sorry, but I'll need this one." I kept the .380 in my hand. "Your face is a mess," I told Givens.

"No thanks to you," he muttered.

"I did all that? Just by pushing open the door? Wow. I had no idea I could multitask so well."

Givens touched his split lip gingerly with his left hand and whimpered.

"Who did do all that?" I asked.

He didn't reply. The blonde opened her mouth, but he grunted, and she went silent, pouting. It was an impressive exchange.

203

"I don't think they want to talk," Mike said.

"They're afraid."

The babe said, "Huh?"

"Just talking to myself. I do that when I'm confused. And when I'm angry. I even do it before I use my gun on someone." I held it up. The blonde squealed, twisting around and showing me her back. A sprig of holly showed brightly on her left shoulder blade, as well as a string of rose petals spanning her lower back. I wanted to see what she had on her ass but knew that wouldn't go over too well with Mike. I didn't care how Givens felt about it.

When I finally got around to pulling my gaze away from her, I noticed that Givens had straightened in his seat. His eyes bulged and his bloody mouth was wide open. It was an unflattering—and disgusting—sight.

"Close your mouth," I said.

He did.

"All right, here's the deal. I know what's going on and I know you're involved. If you want me to leave you two alone, you'd better answer my questions. Got it?"

Givens didn't reply. The blonde nodded. I knew she'd talk; she was scared enough. Women aren't as stubborn as men when threatened with death or disfigurement.

"Who are you working for?"

Silence.

"Okay. If you really want to go this route. . ." I stood. "Either of you ever seen someone who's just been pistol-whipped?"

The blonde gasped. Givens stiffened in his seat; his mouth dropped open again.

I was relieved by their reactions. There was no way I could pistol-whip anyone. That would involve having one of those genes violent criminals had. I lacked such a gene.

But in this case, the mere threat was all I needed.

I held up the revolver. "This one's small, but the front sight is kind of sharp."

The blonde trembled. Some platinum hair slid down her left arm.

"Whaddya want, man?" Givens asked, his voice whiny.

"Just a couple of answers and I'll go. Imagine that. Five minutes from now, I'll be long gone, and the two of you can finish whatever you were doing when I came in."

"I can't talk to ya, man. They'll kill me."

"Who?"

Silence.

I took a step and raised the revolver.

"You're not going to actually *do* that, are you?" Mike asked.

I gave her a quick wink and turned to the blonde, hoping she'd help me out.

"He works at V-Vesper's!" she blurted out. "So . . . do I! I-I d-dance there--"

"God*dammm*it, Trina!" Givens sat bolt upright. "You're gonna get us *both* killed!"

"Keep going. This is getting interesting."

"That's it, Mister." Apparently his fear of his comrades had won out over the fear of a pistol-whipping. This told me quite a bit. "Nothin' else, understand? That's all we're saying. So if you wanna--"

"He's one of the bouncers," Trina said. "He's a real jerk, too, always trying to cop a feel with the girls."

"What's his name?"

"Tank," she said. "Everyone calls him Tank. They really should call him Godzilla. Or Gorilla--"

"I get it. So what's the setup?"

"Listen, man." Givens' face had turned pale. "I can't tell you anything--understand? I'll end up in a dumpster with my throat slashed!"

"You listen. And try to pay attention. You're blown. You and your buds are in deep shit. We're talking murder, conspiracy--"

"M-Murder?" His eyes bulged.

"We both know your roommate's in this just as deep as--"

"He's dead," the blonde said quickly.

Givens gawked at her. He turned to me. "I didn't kill Berto! I swear to God!"

I didn't want to tell him I knew about the spiked drink. Telling him about Mike's discovery would send him over the edge.

"Ever heard of accessory after the fact? That means you'll go down with the guy who actually

206

did the murder. And even if you don't, once Papa Joe finds out what you've been doing, he'll send a few of his people looking for you. In other words, if you don't play ball with me, you're going down hard."

He'd cringed when I mentioned Raguzzo's name. "I'm fucked . . . no matter *what* I do!"

I tried a gamble. "Who held the gun to your head and told you to look the other way when a couple of packages walked away just before you made your trip to Biloxi?"

"Listen, man, all they did was--" He stopped, turned pale again. "How the fuck . . . h-how'd you--"

"Never mind how. You did this to yourself, and if your girlfriend has any brains, she'll get the hell out before they think she was involved. And if you're smart, you'll tell me what you know. Maybe I'll tell Raguzzo you were too stupid to realize what was actually going on. Maybe he'll believe it, maybe not. But it's the only chance you've got. If Raguzzo knows you cooperated, he just might forget about you and turn to the others. Anyone can tell you're small potatoes. Raguzzo cares only about the brains here--the big shots that made all the plans, the arrangements. But even if Papa Joe doesn't care about you, you're still gonna have a bunch of folks after you. You'll have to consider a major move. I suggest a different part of the country. Maybe even South America. Shave your head and change your name. It sucks, but it'll be much better than being carted off to a dumpster with your throat slashed."

"I . . . dunno, man. . ."

"He knows, Mister." Trina had recovered. The glare she'd just given her boyfriend made him squirm. She turned to me. "Tell us what you want from us."

"All I want is a couple of names."

"Shit!" Givens groaned. "*That's* my way out?"

"What do you expect when you cuddle up with psychos? You might stand a snowball's chance of getting out of this--that is, if you're telling me the truth and had nothing to do with murdering Shields. Then again, you might get your throat slashed anyway. These folks aren't exactly the type to forgive and forget. Then there are the cops, who frown on murder. They don't forgive or forget, either."

"I didn't kill him, I swear! I was there--I admit it. The three of us were talking about . . . well, we were just talking, and--"

"What were you talking about?"

"Nothing, man." Givens sat forward and scratched the back of his neck. "It . . . doesn't matter."

"It matters if you were talking about me."

He groaned, shifting in his seat. The groan told me one thing, the shifting another. He looked just about as guilty as someone with their hand in the cash register. He suddenly took a deep breath, and I knew I was about to hear more lies. "Why would we be talkin' . . . about you?"

"You still think I don't know what's going on?"

208

Givens rubbed his eyes again. "All right, all right. The three of us--"

"You, Shields, and who else?"

Givens moaned. "I . . . can't *tell* you his name."

"All right, I'll let that go for now. Go on."

"We were talking about you--"

"At the place on 39th?"

Givens sucked in a gasp. He gawked at me as if I'd just grown another ear. "How the fuck did you know--"

"You just told me. But do go on."

It took him a while to recover. He slumped in his seat the way people do when they realize all is lost. "I was told to go out there and wait for Berto to join us. I went there with—with this other guy. We were talking--"

"About what?"

"It was about those two college geeks Berto hired to take you on a ride."

"Then what?"

He threw up his arms. "I dunno, man! Berto really fucked up, and the guy we were with, well, he just lit into him."

"Then you and this other guy killed Shields."

"No! It wasn't like that! Berto just . . . he just . . . fainted. Dropped dead."

"Did he have a heart problem?"

"I dunno, man. I was his bud. I ain't no damn doctor."

"He just keeled over and died? Just like that?"

"Just like that."

"And neither of you two helped him to the floor?"

"Hell no, man! I ain't no killer!"

"You're trying to tell me you just made the drinks, and a minute later, your friend keeled over and died?"

"Yeah, man. The other guy . . . he . . . he handed Berto--" Givens rubbed his eyes and shook his head. "Shit. He did something . . . to Berto's drink. Fuck, man . . ."

"It happened that way," Mike said.

"Okay. I believe you. Now all you have to worry about is Papa Joe figuring out who he wants to go after. At least you don't have to face a murder charge."

Givens' face had turned bone white. "Like I said, I'm fucked--no matter what."

"You should've thought of that before all this started."

"Berto . . . he said it was no big thing. Papa Joe . . . he's got more shit than he knows what to do with. He wouldn't even miss it. . . ."

"Agreed."

He stared curiously at me. "Then . . . you know why we did it?"

"Yeah. I know why you did it. What did you get out of it? A couple of grand?"

Givens sighed. "Five hundred."

Five hundred bucks to mess up your life. Beard and Blondie had done it for even less. What was wrong with the brain activity in these upcoming generations?

"You really are stupid." I couldn't believe this.

"Tell me something I don't know. But I ain't no killer. And Berto was my bud. . ."

"Then you won't mind telling me that other man's name."

"If I give it to you, I'll be dead in three--"

"We don't know his name," Trina said quickly.

"Then how do you know him?"

"He comes into the club all the time."

"Dammit, Trina. You're *killin'* me!"

"He comes in on Fridays and Saturdays. He's a real creep, but he dresses well and gives us twenties for lap dances. A couple of the girls like him. He thinks he's hot stuff--"

"Shut up, Trina!"

"You shut up, Givens. You want your girlfriend going down for this, too?"

"One of the girls said he owns pawnshops in Kissimmee." Trina pushed some hair away from her face, but it came right back, brushing the side of her right boob. It was all I could do to remember where her face was. "He's got black hair and he's always touching it--you know, like he's making sure it's perfect. But he's really creepy, the way he looks at us."

"He was the other guy I saw at the house," Mike said.

Black hair. Vain. And Mike said he sounded Spanish. The pawnshops in Kissimmee narrowed it down, but I had to make sure. "Is this guy Italian?"

"He's a *Spic*." Trina practically spat out the word.

211

"You're sure about that?"

"I can tell the difference between Spics and Dagos."

"What am I?"

She swallowed. "You're . . . not Hispanic, are ya?"

"I thought you said you could tell."

"I can. Most of the time. You look . . . Italian, maybe?" She squirmed and ran both hands through her hair.

"Right on the money."

She seemed to loosen up. "I've always liked Italian guys."

I found myself staring at those boobs again . . .

"You two want a room?" Mike asked flatly.

Dammit . . . At this rate, I'd need hosed down. I rubbed my temples. *Pay attention, now.* "And you say he comes into Vesper's on Fridays and Saturdays?"

"We see him there just about every week."

"What time's he usually come in?"

"Around ten, ten-thirty. Sometimes later."

I turned back to Givens. I had to find out about the men in the black Audi. "Now tell me about those three men."

He swallowed loudly. "W-What three men?"

"Tell him, Paul." She was glaring again. "If you won't, I will."

He sighed and sank back into the cushions. "They . . . work for this guy. They're--"

"They're wet boys. Yeah, I got that. Did they once work for Raguzzo?"

He shrugged.

"I'm not gonna ask you again."

"One of them. Still does, I think. They call him Bear. The others, they work for someone else."

"Who?"

"Some big shot Hispanic, owns a shitload of places in Kissimmee."

"Paseo?"

He turned even whiter. "H-How do you know--"

"Never mind." It was time to go. I'd learned enough from Givens. "You working tonight?" I asked Trina.

She touched her cheek and frowned. "Fat chance of that. . ." She shot Givens a glare.

I'd originally thought their visitors had roughed them both up. Her glare told me I was wrong. "*You* did that?"

He shrugged. "She pissed me off."

"Know what pisses *me* off?" I stood. "Assholes who beat up women."

Givens slumped forward and covered his face.

I held out the revolver for her. "You want this? It might make you feel better."

She shook her head. "What I'm gonna do will be even better."

"You mean what you're *not* gonna do?"

"You got it, Mister."

Chapter Seventeen

At ten o'clock, Vesper's was packed.

I parked about a dozen rows down from the front and sat in the car, watching the bouncers handle the small crowd at the door.

"He's kind of bold, isn't he?" Mike said. "The guy who killed Shields."

"Yeah, I've never been able to figure out how certain people have no qualms about killing others."

"I was talking about that other thing he does."

"You mean how he comes here and gets his rocks off with the lap dance babes while putting the screws to Papa Joe's organization at the same time?"

"I wanted to phrase it a little better, but yeah, that's it in a nutshell."

"You're right. He's quite a character."

"You really think he's working for that other guy? The Hispanic who kidnapped you last year? Or could he be going behind that guy's back, too?"

"It's possible, although I doubt it. Paseo and Papa Joe have a mutual respect for one another and won't shit in one another's yard."

"Is this an honor-among-thieves thing?"

"It's more of a mutual fear. Papa Joe knows that if he bites Paseo in the ass, it'll start a war. Both men would have to watch their backs forever. However, if Papa Joe does him a favor, Paseo'll owe him. They're crooks, but they're also respectable businessmen."

214

"That sounds more reasonable."

"Raguzzo's as honorable as they come, I guess. But I still wouldn't trust any of them. They're all unpredictable."

"So what's your plan?"

"Look around inside, find the guy with the hair, follow him outside, check out what vehicle he gets into and follow him again."

"Without getting too close, of course."

"Of course."

"And how will you do that?"

"I won't."

"I guess this is where I come in?"

"Exactly." My nerves shook as I put my .380 in my console.

"No gun?"

"No gun."

"You don't want them to accidentally discover it while you're in there, right?"

"That's basically it."

"What'll they do?"

"Drive me somewhere, shoot me with it, and dump my body."

"I think you're doing the right thing, keeping it in the car."

"Thanks. It seems sensible to me as well."

***

I handed over a ten-spot at the door and wondered if either of the two slabs of muscle was Tank or Bear.

Both easily qualified, but all the bouncers working here would qualify as well. I focused on the crowd as I went inside, hoping Mike would be able to spot our Man of the Hour.

I edged through the crowd, stopping to let one of the scantily clad waitresses squeeze by. Mike moved in a straight line, through knots of well-dressed men sipping drinks.

I wondered what people would think if they knew a dead babe was walking through them. It would probably freak them out. Most people don't react very well to ghosts or the afterlife.

I glanced at my watch. 10:15. As far as I could tell, Black Hair hadn't followed me in. He might already be here. I hoped he hadn't deviated from his routine and skipped coming here.

I didn't want to drink while I was working but didn't have much of a choice. Someone would approach me within five minutes if I didn't soon have a glass in my hand.

I squeezed through staggered clots of grinning customers, heading straight for the L-shaped bar. I ordered a vodka gimlet from the tall redheaded barmaid. I chose the gimlet because I hated its taste and wouldn't drink it--but at least no one could accuse me of not buying anything.

I paid and turned away from the bar. Mike appeared through a couple of fat men in suits, drifting right over. "He's here," she said above the thundering sound system.

"Where?"

She pointed toward the hall leading to the lap dancing area.

I followed a pair of well-dressed exec-type guys past the restrooms, a door marked *CONVENTION A*, and another marked *CONFERENCE ROOM*. At the end of the well-lit hall, lush maroon drapes sealed off a wide archway. Standing off to the side, a mountain of flesh in a dark suit stretched at the seams watched us closely. He pulled the drape aside just enough to let us enter in single file, releasing it just as I cleared the doorway. The heavy curtain slapped me on the back, urging me inside.

The lap dancing area, about half the size of the main room, fluttered with multicolored lights fitted into recessed domes in the concave ceiling. Six naked, large-breasted babes in open-toed silver spikes danced seductively around men sitting on chairs, in time with the pulsating African-type drumbeat.

A small crowd had gathered farther down in six separate lines, awaiting their turn. I counted about twelve guys in front of me. Their expressions were all the same--thirsty, horny, and desperate to relieve themselves of cash and inhibitions.

"He's over there," Mike whispered. "The left side of the room. In the chair near the drapes."

I shifted my position for a better view. Since his back faced me, I couldn't see his face. Trina had been right about his hair. Black, wavy and thick, professionally cut and styled. Not one hair was out of place. When the blond stripper threatened to touch it, he held up an index finger and shook his head.

"Talk about vanity," I said.

"Trina was right," Mike said.

When the dance finished, Black Hair got up. He stuffed another bill down the stripper's G-string and touched his hair carefully at the crown before heading back to the entrance.

I waited for him to pass. As he did, I got a better look. About six-two. Good-looking. A meticulous dresser. A Rolex watch. Two gold bracelets. A silver ear stud and several rings on each hand. He was definitely Hispanic and liked spending money on himself.

I waited about twenty seconds before turning around and groping my way back out. Just as I re-entered the hall lighting, I lost him in the huge crowd swarming at the hall entrance.

Mike drifted over. "He's outside."

Dammit. I'd obviously waited too long.

I squeezed through the crowd and set my glass on the tray of a passing waitress. Just as one of the double doors opened from the outside, I elbowed through the small crowd gathered at the entrance.

The parking lot was a nightmare. Vehicles trudged up and down the aisles, searching for available spaces. Some passed by the front of the building slowly, hoping for a closer spot. Small groups marched eagerly toward the building while others staggered back to their rides.

The spotlights at the corner of the building helped a little, but I had no idea where Black Hair was. I didn't see the black Mercedes anywhere close to the building. I suspected someone like him would own more than one prime ride and would drive here in something he'd want to show off. I also suspected he'd park near the building, possibly in the *Reserved* section, so I concentrated on the front two aisles.

"Over there." Mike had appeared beside me again, pointing to our right, where a slim figure had slipped behind the wheel of a black Corvette parked at the far end of the first row.

Prime ride, indeed. Sometimes I amazed myself.

I rushed down the paved slope in that direction, hoping to get a fix on the tag, but as soon as I squeezed between two sports cars fighting for the same space, the Vette's lights came on. The sleek ride pulled out and hurried down the aisle, away from me.

Damn. I had to get back to the TransAm. It was parked in the next aisle. I didn't have much time. Once Black Hair got on the Trail, he'd be gone in a flash.

I started to turn.

"Don't move." Something hard pressed into my lower back.

I started to raise my hands.

"I *said*, don't move!"

I froze.

"Goin' somewhere?" I could tell whoever was behind me was huge. His bored, low-pitched voice sounded like it was at least a foot above my head.

"Not with that gun sticking in my back."

"Where's your ride?"

"Over there."

"Where?"

"About ten rows down, on the left."

"Point."

"You told me not to move."

"*Point*, asshole."

I pointed.

"Start walkin'." The gun tapped me harder.

***

As soon as we reached my car, he poked me in the lower back again. "Get in."

"I have to get my keys."

"Get 'em."

I reached into my pocket.

Just then, I heard Mike's voice about five feet away, coming from my left. "Hi, big guy. Wanna party?"

The pressure on my lower back vanished. I felt him shifting his weight on the gravel.

I turned. Assuming her solid form, Mike appeared about ten feet away, in bra and panties. Smiling at the huge guy behind me, she played with her hair, taking a thick strand of it and letting it slide across her left breast.

I couldn't believe what I was seeing. My attention shifted abruptly.

Mike's voice snapped me out of it. "Focus," she said flatly.

I grabbed the automatic from the gorilla's huge paw while Mike faded into the darkness. The big ape realized he'd been imagining things and gawked at his empty hand. I brought the gun up, cracking him on the chin. He stepped back, glaring at me. I

220

slammed my elbow into his gut. It had no effect, so I jumped up and cracked him on the forehead with the gun. It drove a grunt from his throat, but he didn't go down. I gave the same spot another brutal swat. This time, he went down.

My limbs trembled as I released the clip from the big ape's piece. I lobbed the empty gun beneath the low rider parked next to the TransAm and tossed the clip in the bushes.

A short line of vehicles waited at the lighted entrance. I couldn't tell if the black Corvette was among them, but if I was lucky, I might be able to get there in time.

I jumped in, fired up and shot down the aisle. I pulled out at the far end, and had no problem reaching the main entrance.

The Corvette had already gone.

***

Mike appeared beside me in the seat.

No bra and panties this time--just her red tee shirt and Capri's. Knowing her as I did, I probably wouldn't see her like that again for quite a while.

"He turned left and went south," she said.

I tried tossing the image of my dead half-naked buddy to the back of my mind and forced myself to focus on the black Vette. It was tough, but my adrenaline helped me through it.

"You're sure?"

"Positive. I also caught his tag number."

My heart thumped heavily. "That's huge."

"It's C-A-R-D-O R-O-X."

I wanted to kiss her. "Damn, I wish you weren't dead."

"Why?"

"So I could kiss you."

"But . . . if I wasn't dead, I couldn't--"

"I know."

"And I wouldn't be able to--"

"I know."

"And you wouldn't be able to--"

"I know that, too."

She sighed. "I guess I need to stop trying to make sense when I'm around you."

"I keep hoping you'll eventually figure that out." I forced the big car into the heavy southbound traffic.

***

Twenty minutes later, the black Vette made a quick left onto 39th Street.

"I should've suspected." My heart raced.

"I'll bet they're getting ready for a shipment tonight," Mike said.

"Whatever they're doing, I'd better be there to see it." I made the left at the light and pulled into the parking lot of the apartment complex across the street from the filling station, coasting down three aisles and selecting a space far enough away from the turnoff so the TransAm wouldn't be spotted. Before I got out, I slipped my .380 into my jacket pocket and made sure my cell phone was easily accessible.

"You gonna call someone?" Mike asked.

"Take pictures. Hopefully, I'll have enough light to do it."

"I'll let you know what's going on as soon as I can."

"I'll probably be sneaking around close by."

"Just be careful. You can't afford to get caught."

"I know. One other thing."

"What's that?"

"You looked really hot in your bra and panties."

She frowned. "Apparently *too* hot, judging by how you instantly turned into a zombie."

"I gotta work on my self-control one of these days."

"You'd better. That guy was going to kill you."

"He didn't get the chance. I snapped out of it in time."

"Only because I told you to."

"You're my guardian angel. Saving me is what you do."

"That doesn't mean you've got to make my job any harder than it already is."

"What can I say? Testosterone can be a problem."

"For women, too."

"It doesn't help when you flash all that good stuff at me."

"Need I remind you that all that good stuff is dead? Besides, I wasn't flashing it at you, I was flashing it at that other guy. The one holding the gun on you."

"Doesn't matter. I managed to catch a healthy eyeful, as well."

"Oh, stop. We've got work to do." She disappeared in the darkness.

I crossed the lot and crept down the walk, keeping close to the bushes while watching out for passing traffic. It was a quiet neighborhood, and since it was getting late, the only traffic I heard roared down the Trail a safe distance behind me. Whoever owned this piece of property had selected it for its privacy and seclusion.

As I drew closer to the house, the mashing of leaves drifted over in the night air, on the other side of the bushes. Hunkering down, I edged into them, concealing myself. The beam of a flashlight passed over the top of the bushes, moving along the walk, as far down the block as it could reach. It came back moments later, scouring the bushes again, before moving in the opposite direction. After about a minute, it died when the flashlight clicked off.

The mashing of leaves again, moving away.

Wonderful silence filled the cool air.

Mike appeared beside me. "They know you're coming," she whispered. "That huge guy you knocked out at the club. That was Tank, and he called them here as soon as he came to."

"I should've swatted that bastard a third time."

"Or at least taken his cell phone."

"That would've worked, too."

"Anyway, the guard with the flashlight went back to the storage building. They make their rounds at regular intervals but will probably do it more frequently if they think you're wandering around. The cameras are on, but there's a blind spot over there, close to where the bushes separate. The cameras miss it by about two feet."

"Where is everyone?"

"In the house. There's a van coming in a few minutes, but if you hurry, you might have time to reach the house."

"Can you help me make it to the house?"

She sighed. "You're not . . . going inside, are you?"

I couldn't believe she'd just asked me that. "I'm not a *total* idiot."

She shook her head. "Sometimes I wonder . . ."

"About my being a total idiot?"

"About what you're gonna do, silly."

"I'll be satisfied if I can reach a window. Even if I do, I might not be able to take a clear picture. But I've got to try. Getting to the house alive will be a good start."

"You can't make it without my help. But you've got to follow me closely, understand?"

"No problem."

"It's a straight shot. It cuts diagonally across the front yard."

"You lead. I'll follow."

Chapter Eighteen

Keeping low, I followed her hazy image as it moved in a straight line, toward the left side of the house, where the shuttered window glowed with an orange light above an unruly growth of bushes.

I scoured the grounds as I moved in the grass, alert for any signs of movement penetrating the darkness behind the house, or from the direction of the storage building. The spots lit up both sides of the house, a small portion of the front lawn and the area in back. The route Mike used was cloaked in darkness, with only a weak yellow curtain reaching across the section that ended just a few feet from the bushes in front of the property.

I finally reached the bushes in front of the shuttered window, squeezing between them and using a thick section to conceal my body. Just as I settled amongst them, I heard the mashing of leaves.

Someone was walking down the path, about ten feet from the house. I squatted behind my bush and held my breath.

The footsteps stopped. So did my heart. I didn't move.

"C'mon out," said a bored, low-pitched voice.

A flashlight clicked on, its beam moving along the top of the bush in front of me. I continued holding my breath.

The clicking of a gun hammer.

I nearly emptied my bladder.

"I'll count to three," the voice said, still sounding bored.

My heart sputtered. *Damn*. I didn't have much of a choice. My only chance was to try and get him before he got me. It shouldn't be that much of a problem; he was only a few feet away. I might even be able to hit him.

But what about the other guard? Were there more than one? The others in the house would hear the gunshot and would be out here in seconds.

Still, I had no choice. My hand inched toward the gun in my pocket.

"He's bluffing," Mike whispered.

I risked turning my head in her direction. She winked, suggesting she knew what she was talking about. Still, the urge to grab my gun was overwhelming.

"Trust me," she said.

That was all I needed to hear. Mike had a much better view and a better grasp of the situation. I didn't move.

About thirty agonizing seconds later, the flashlight beam clicked off. Another *click* of the gun hammer, this time easing back, caused my pulse to skip a couple of beats.

Silence. The footsteps grew fainter as they moved away.

"You're okay now," Mike whispered.

I waited for my heart to start working again. I checked my pants. Dry. I'd probably grown a few gray hairs, but that was no big deal. That's why God made Grecian Formula. The important thing was that I hadn't wet my pants. Wet pants would be definitely put a crimp in my plans. I slowly straightened and crept closer to the side window.

On the other side of the sheer white drapes, three men stood in the center of the shabbily furnished living room. Black Hair, a drink in his hand, leaned against the fireplace. The second man--medium height, bulky and bald--stood in the center of the room, talking softly. The third man was tall and slender, with large dark eyes, heavy brows, and his head shaved to the bone. He also held a drink but spoke only when the bald man sipped his drink. He looked familiar, but I had too much else on my mind to go on a sudden trip down Memory Lane.

Since the window was closed, I could hear only soft mumbling. I pressed my ear against the cool stucco wall. It didn't help.

"Mike? You still here?"

"Of course."

"Do me a favor and find out what they're saying, okay?"

"No problem."

I pulled my cell from my pants pocket. It was an IPhone and took great pictures. I made sure the flash was off. It was a gamble, but I couldn't risk being seen, and hoped the camera could produce acceptable images using only the living room lighting.

I snapped six shots before I heard footfalls again. I sunk back down into my deep squat position and waited, my ears pricked.

A flashlight beam swept across the side of the house, just above the bushes. My heart raced. The beam swept across the bushes again, this time lower. I lowered my head and pushed my face closer into the bushes.

The flashlight beam vanished.

I waited a full minute before moving. Then I straightened and peered into the room. The men had gone.

About a minute later, the quiet whine of a van grew louder as it cruised down the street. It slowed in front of the house, pulled into the drive, and stopped in front of the storage building, where the Vette, a silver Charger, and a black Jaguar were parked. The driver got out and vanished in the darkness. A moment later, the spot above the entrance came on, illuminating the man's face and dark clothing.

I moved between bushes and aimed my IPhone. Using the zoom lens, I tried focusing, but the darkness--as well as the distance--was too much for the digital camera. I'd have to rely on my memory to relate what I saw.

A large man wearing a shoulder holster came out of the building and stood beneath the spot, talking to the driver. A moment later, he went back inside. The humming sound of a garage door drifted over. I assumed it must have been directly behind the van. Its driver disappeared behind the van, and a metal door slid open.

I still couldn't see anything but was forced to stay right where I was. I couldn't even take pictures of the vehicles because of the distance and horrible lighting.

Mike reappeared beside me. "They're loading those packages now."

"I wish I could see."

"I'll go back and see how they're doing. Don't move." She vanished again.

A few minutes later, the driver got back in the van, turned around and went back down the drive. He pulled out and headed west.

I wanted to run back to the TransAm and follow but knew I'd better stay here until Mike told me it was safe to leave.

I waited about ten minutes. Black Hair left the house through a side door, followed by the other two. They chatted briefly and separated, each returning to their rides. Black Hair got in his Vette. The tall slender man slid into the Charger and the bald guy got behind the wheel of the Jag.

Not long after, all I could hear was a loud, obnoxious cicada and the traffic on South Orange Blossom Trail.

Mike returned. "It's time to go."

"What about the guard?"

"There are two of them. They're in the storage building, playing cards."

"Aren't they watching the cameras?"

"They don't seem to be concerned."

She was probably right. Whatever happened had gone down without a hitch. The guards wouldn't be expecting trouble from now on.

***

It was late by the time I got back to my apartment on Conway.

I was tired and hungry, and needed a strong drink. But I knew better than lower my guard as I got out of the TransAm. You never lower your guard when dealing with mob guys. I'd messed up their plans several times in the last couple of days and didn't want to do anything stupid at this stage. Besides, I didn't want anything bad to happen before I reported my findings to Papa Joe. Or before I was able to spend all the money I'd just earned.

I closed the door of the TransAm and pulled the .380 out of my jacket.

Mike drifted over. "It's all right," she said. "There's no one in your apartment, and the parking lot's pretty deserted."

Relieved, I crossed the road and went up the short slope to my front door. I unlocked it and opened it. This time, I waited until Mike went in first. I still felt guilty about slamming it in her face that last time.

As always, I went straight to the kitchen and fixed a drink. "By the way, how did you know that guy was bluffing? The one pointing the flashlight at the bush I was hiding in." It had been bugging me since I'd left 39th Street.

"He wasn't aiming the gun at you, he had it pointed at the ground."

That made no sense. "That doesn't mean he was bluffing."

Mike shrugged. "He just didn't look serious . . ."

"How'd he look?"

"Bored. I could tell he didn't want to be out there. I think he wanted to be back in the storage building, playing cards."

Somehow, that wasn't the answer I was looking for.

"I was right, wasn't I?"

"Yeah . . ."

"He didn't shoot you, did he?"

"No . . ."

"Then stop with all the questions. I know what I'm doing."

I knew better than argue. "Okay . . . so tell me what happened back there. Things I need to know."

"The guards were the ones who tried to kill you last night."

"Those guards are wet boys?"

"Apparently."

"What about the guy who showed up in the van?"

"They didn't say much. They just went inside and pulled open one of the doors. They had a pallet of those packages ready. About ten packages."

Ten packages of coke. Going by the size and description Mike had given me, the street value would be well over a million.

"As soon as they'd helped load up, the driver got back in the van, talked to someone named Tuco and said he'd be about twenty minutes."

"Did you hear Tuco say anything?"

"He said he'd have his boys ready for the shipment and reminded the driver to return the van to the dealership and take off the dummy tags."

"What went on in the house?"

"As I told you, they were all worried about what happened outside the club. They didn't like it that you got away from that Tank character. The one with the black hair--his name is Salazar--he assured the other two he wasn't followed when he left the club."

"Did you get the names of the other two?"

"They called the bald man Marko. They called the Salazar guy Ricardo, but no one called the third man anything. He didn't say much."

Once again I combed my memory. The shaved scalp and dark eyes struck a nerve, but I just couldn't place the man. "Nothing rings a bell, but it's better than nothing."

"Anyway, they were discussing what they should do with you if you showed up at the house. Salazar said the guards should take you to Kissimmee and leave your corpse for Paseo. They could hit one of his stores and make it look like you did it. That would get Paseo after Papa Joe, and a war would weed out the dead wood and decide who should really be running Orlando. Marko wanted to knock you out and frame you for the murder of Salvatore somebody. Know anyone by that name?"

"I believe someone named Salvatore handles the books from Raguzzo's out-of-town ventures. He might possibly be the one balancing the accounts from Raguzzo's casinos. If these people are skimming, Salvatore will find out pretty soon. These guys would consider him a huge threat."

"Marko said he thought it unforgivable that Raguzzo didn't kill you when he had the chance, and thought that car bomb thing was a hoax."

"It looked real to me."

"It was real, but Marko says it was staged to make it look like he'd actually tried nailing you."

"What would be the sense in that?"

"He said Papa Joe wanted it to look like you were really good for spotting it. Getting a top-notch private eye on the payroll, one who got along with the cops, could be good for business. But it didn't look like you were working for the Mob at all, and Papa Joe had made a big mistake by not having you killed. You were a threat and Papa Joe couldn't even see that. Papa Joe was getting soft and stupid, and much too old to run things anymore."

"How about the third guy?"

"He wanted to pay an out-of-town hitter to kill you and dump your body."

"I seem to be making a lot of enemies lately. Maybe if I smiled more? Had the bad guys over for poker and beer? Tried another line of work? Read a book or two on etiquette?"

"I can't see you doing any of that."

"Neither can I."

"Anyway, they decided to forget about you for the time being. They didn't want anything to interfere with their weekly shipments, and as long as no one knew what they were doing, they could

234

keep on doing it. But if you got any closer, they'd kill you."

"Actually, I don't need to get any closer. Thanks to you, I've got names, details, an address, and some good shots of the bad guys. I don't need anything else."

"Is there any chance they'll send someone else after you anyway?"

"There's always a chance of that. But since the bad guys are probably convinced I don't know anything, I'm not a threat anymore."

"What about Givens? He won't tell them about you, will he?"

"If he has any sense at all, he's long gone."

Chapter Nineteen - Sunday

After a restful night, I called Vesper's a few minutes after one o'clock the following afternoon. I'd wanted to call earlier, but Vesper's didn't open until one on Sundays.

I didn't expect to talk to Sonny; he usually didn't come in until after two on Sundays. Giorgio Matteo's soft, pleasant voice served as a welcome substitute to Sonny's usual harsh bellowing.

"How can I help you, Mister Deacon?"

Mister Deacon. I liked that. It made me realize there was order to the world after all. It promised to be a sunny day, my biorhythm was up, I'd survived another night, and tomorrow morning, I'd make my bank account fat and happy.

Life was good.

"I need to talk to Papa Joe. I know he's probably at Mass, so could you please leave a message for him? This is very important."

"I'll give him the message. If he's at noon Mass, he should be able to respond shortly."

"While I've got you on the line, I wonder if you could tell me something."

"If I can."

"You know someone named Marko?"

"Marko Rossi manages Dante's, if that's who you mean."

This wasn't good. This wasn't good at all.

"Does he run it alone?"

"He's the executive manager. The assistant manager, Dale Kobe, does all the ordering, and manages all food and beverage shipments. Dale's really on the ball, and has a good head for business. He even convinced Papa Joe buy a fish market in Bay St. Louis to make sure the two casinos--as well as Dante's--get only the freshest catches from the Gulf."

"Describe Kobe."

"Dale's around forty. He's tall—about six-four, I guess—with dark eyes--"

"A shaved head?"

"Yes. Is any of this significant? I know this is a confidential matter, but--"

"Just tossing around ideas." This was getting progressively worse. Papa Joe was not going to have a good day.

"I'll give the boss your message."

"Thanks."

While I waited, I poured another cup of coffee, went into the living room. I stuck an old Maynard Ferguson CD in the player. His Newport album from the mid-sixties. It was a great album. The type of music that stirs you up, makes you feel good inside.

I *should* feel good. In just two days I'd survived two murder attempts and two kidnapping attempts, and earned a huge chunk of change along the way.

But I knew I shouldn't feel *too* triumphant. Mike was the one who'd helped me solve the case. Without her, I would have been killed, or at least left to die in the trunk of my car.

237

My cell buzzed.

I muted the volume on Maynard and glanced at my watch. It was one-thirty. The display said *Unknown name, unknown number*.

"You got something for me this morning?" the raspy voice asked. "Or more questions?"

"I have only one. Where can we meet?"

"You *got* something?"

"I solved the case, but I've got to meet you somewhere private."

"How about Dante's?"

Judging by what I'd just learned from Giorgio, I didn't want to go there at all. "Try another place."

"What's wrong with Dante's?"

"I'll tell you when I see you."

A silence. Papa Joe was wondering what was going on, why I didn't want to meet him at his favorite eating place. I could almost see him frowning, rubbing his forehead. Listening to my silence to pick something up from it.

"You at your place right now?"

"Yeah."

"Gimme an hour. I'll have one of my men pick you up."

***

Precisely one hour later, I heard someone outside.

I crept up to the peephole. A gray Town Car with darkly tinted windows sat along the curb in front of my apartment. A tall, broad-shouldered man in a dark suit and a black chauffeur's cap got out from behind the wheel and came up the walk. It was

238

the same guy who'd taken me to Dante's in the limo the other night.

The doorbell buzzed.

I didn't have Mike with me this time, so I had to be extra careful. Keeping the chain on, I placed my foot about six inches from the edge of the door and unlocked it, easing it open.

"Yes?"

"I've come to pick you up, Mister Deacon."

Yep, the same guy. But that didn't mean I was safe. This could be another trap. The bad guys could have bought him off and told him to pick me up so he could dump me somewhere. I knew I could be way off, but I'd rather be paranoid and safe than lower my guard and end up dead.

I remembered the drill from our last encounter. "What's your mother's name?"

"George."

He remembered. This was good. Still, I was hesitant.

"He's okay." Mike slipped through the door in her cream blouse, cutoff jeans and red tennies. Her hair was tied in a knot. She looked playful and tomboyish. "The mob guy's in the car, waiting. He keeps looking at his watch. I don't think he likes to be kept waiting."

"Really?" I couldn't believe Papa Joe had paid me a personal visit.

"It's what we agreed on, sir," the chauffeur said flatly.

"Right." For a moment I'd forgotten about him. "Yeah. Sure. Listen . . . I'll be out in a minute."

239

"Make it quick, all right?" The chauffeur's face tightened. He'd probably be fired or at least chewed out if I didn't come right out with him.

"One sec."

"And please leave your piece."

"No prob." I closed the door and picked up my IPhone from the kitchen counter. I shot Mike a quick worried look as I took the chain off and opened the door.

"What the hell kept ya?" Papa Joe glared as I got in beside him. He wore a dark suit and white silk shirt, but no tie. As compensation, he'd stuck a fresh white carnation in his lapel. His cologne smelled pricey. He'd probably come straight from church.

"I had to make sure it was okay." I settled comfortably in the lush leather seat while the chauffeur closed my door. He opened his own door and slid behind the wheel. Mike appeared on Raguzzo's other side. "I've made a few enemies in the last day or so," I added.

The Town Car eased away so smoothly, I hardly noticed.

"Try running an organization," he said gruffly.

"Not a chance. I irritate people too much."

"You can say that again."

"Okay . . . Not a chance. I irritate--"

"Smartass. So tell me . . . whaddya got?"

I took out my IPhone, got the pictures ready, and handed it over. He took it and began studying them, frowning, grunting, groaning and shaking his head. When he finished, he went through them

240

again, sighed and looked at me. He grimaced and pocketed the cell. "I'll need this."

"Keep it." With the money I was being paid, I could buy another phone.

Papa Joe sat back and was silent for a while. Then, without looking at me, he said, "Tell me the rest."

I told him about 39th Street, and about Shields and Givens. I told him about my visit with Kelly, and also what happened when I tried to see the Gallagher brothers.

Papa Joe took in every word, growing angrier as I spoke, his gnarled fists trembling, a vein in his lined forehead popping out boldly. This was very painful. I was telling him things that hurt, that revealed things about his associates and decisions he'd made in the past. Things that would force him to make choices he didn't want to make.

When I'd finished he said, "The bouncer that suckered you at my club. Describe him."

I did.

Papa Joe shook his head and grunted. "*Stronzone. Inutile idiota.* Lazy *sfachim* was living off his folks when Frankie spotted him at Gold's Gym. His folks told Frankie he was no good. Frankie shoulda listened."

"You can't trust anyone these days," I said. "Especially the young guys."

Papa Joe shook his head. "That don't explain Marko or Dale. They've been with me for years. Marko? I treated him like my own son. He was a punk kid in Miami when I took him in. Sent him to

241

business school, gave him Dante's to run. Dale?" He sighed. "Came to the house every Christmas for years with presents for the grandkids. Uncle Dale, the little ones called him. There ain't no excuse, Deacon. None. *Bastardi*. That's what's taking over now."

"I'm afraid I'm the one they blame for all this."

Papa Joe squinted. "That fucking car bomb?"

"They think you fabricated that story because you wanted me on your payroll. And when they realized I wasn't on the payroll, they considered you weak and senile, and could no longer trust you."

"An excuse, Deacon. They think I'm old. And I am. But I still run things, run 'em damn well. The young, they no understand that little thing you earn as you grow older. It's called wisdom, and it's valuable. More valuable than looks . . . and brains . . . even money. They got no idea, 'cause they no understand what the hell it is. They ain't there yet, and at this rate, they'll never get there."

"That's their problem," I said. "Not ours."

Papa Joe stared at me, trying to penetrate my skull, read what was in there. Something bothered him and he didn't like it, and when something bothered him, he had to find out what it was.

"How'd you do it, Deacon? How'd you get close enough to hear what those *sfachims* were saying? They had guards, right?"

"They were the same two who tried to get me twice before. They needed better."

He was still staring, still trying to read me. My answer didn't explain what he really wanted to

242

know. He was still curious, still relentless. "This don't tell me how you got so close that--"

"You hired me because I'm good, right?"

He nodded.

"I spotted a car bomb no one else could have spotted. You don't think I can get close enough to a bunch of morons and listen in when I want to? Especially when I'm being paid so well?"

"Sometimes you really amaze me," Mike said, smiling next to Papa Joe's face.

"*Touché*." Papa Joe was squinting. "But it still don't tell me how you--"

"You don't really need to know, do you? I mean, how would you like it if a magician told you his secrets?"

"*Si*." He nodded. "You're right. I care only about results."

"Good. We're both wise enough to realize there are some things that should remain a mystery."

His eyes probed me once again. Despite what I'd just told him, he still didn't like it when something was not quite right. I didn't know if it was the businessman in him rationalizing it, the mob boss, or the God-fearing man.

"If I didn't know better, Deacon, I'd think you had a higher power guiding you along."

The God-fearing man had obviously won out.

"Maybe I do," I said. "But if so, I sure wouldn't tell anyone."

"Not even a *paisano*?"

"If I tell anyone, it might not happen again. You know what they say about tempting fate."

"Yep," Mike said, still smiling, "you really are truly amazing."

Silence. Papa Joe's antennae slipped back into his skull. His eyes had changed back, and he was once again viewing the real world. The world of the successful businessman. The mob boss. Back to reality, leaving spirituality where it belonged--in church, or in a nice quiet place of meditation. He'd returned to his own familiar world, where he could talk about things he understood. Things he could explain.

"You've earned your money, Deacon. Twenty-five large will be in your bank account five minutes after the bank opens tomorrow morning."

"You've already given me two K."

He shrugged. "I no recall such a transaction. Where'd this happen?"

I couldn't tell if he was humoring me or if he honestly didn't remember. His eyes revealed nothing. "You don't remember?"

"I'm an old man, and the memory don't work like it used to. Old men like me get confused. Don't confuse me, Deacon."

"Wouldn't think of it." I've never gone out of my way to confuse the elderly.

Chapter Twenty - Monday

Neil Haversack called me promptly at nine the next morning.

I hadn't expected him to call so soon. Usually, it took him most of Monday morning to find out what had happened during the weekend. I suspected Papa Joe had already dealt with the people responsible for threatening his organization. In this case, a body or two might have shown up, and Neil was undoubtedly calling to ask me about it. I didn't know exactly what he'd found out, but if it had something to do with Albert Shields or Paul Givens, he'd want an explanation. Since I'd asked him about Shields, he'd be suspicious.

"What can I do ya for this morning, faithful friend?" I decided on charming and uplifting for my technique. Neil was usually a bear on Monday mornings; a cheerful manner might lift his spirits.

"Drop the bullshit, Deacon. Tell me what's going on."

So much for charming and uplifting . . .

"What's going *on*?" I decided on clueless.

"I wanna know what you've been doing the last two days."

"You mean this weekend?"

"Good guess."

"I was on a case."

"I know that."

"And I've finished."

"I kind of figured that one out, too."

"You seem to know all the answers. I have no idea what else I can tell you."

"You can tell me why a certain stiff is lying in our morgue."

I hated being right about certain things--especially things that could get me in hot water.

"This stiff have a name?"

"Shields. Albert Shields. You called me about him two days ago."

"I remember."

Silence. He was waiting for an explanation. I had a sip of vanilla-flavored coffee to give me a few seconds to figure out what I'd say next. It didn't help.

"I'm waiting, Deacon . . ."

"I know."

"I don't have all day."

"I know that, too."

"Listen to me . . . and try to understand. I'm a cop."

"Is that why they gave you an office in the Police Department?"

"Listen to me, dammit. As a cop, I'm paid to--"

"I know what you're paid to do."

"Then you also know that, as a cop, I'm obligated to investigate homicides, and if I have the teensiest idea about what's going on or who's directly involved, I'm obligated to--"

"I'm not directly involved." I had no choice but go this way. The truth would get me into so much hot water, I didn't think I'd ever be able to come out of it alive.

A pause. Neil was already thinking over my answer, dissecting it. "But you know what happened."

"Actually, I have no idea what happened. When was he killed?"

"Around thirty-six hours ago, going by the M.E.'s report. He was found in a dumpster behind one of the shopping malls on the Trail and Sand Lake Road."

"How was he killed?"

"He had a lethal sedative in his system, and his neck was snapped. Coroner said he was already dead. The head snap was just to make sure."

They more or less had it together--which substantiated what Paul Givens had told me about his part in it. I just couldn't add anything to it without implicating myself and setting myself up for one horrendous afternoon at the Police Station.

"I was in my apartment thirty-six hours ago. A lovely neighbor saw me there, and can vouch for me."

"Could this possibly be the same lovely neighbor who warned you about the two wet boys sneaking into your place Friday night?"

"The very same." I hoped Neil wouldn't want to see her. My options here were limited.

"And you were nowhere near that dumpster?"

"Did they check for prints?"

"You know we did."

"Were mine found anywhere near the dump site?"

"No . . ."

247

"How about on the body?"

A sigh. "Nope."

"How'd you know about the body?"

"An anonymous tip."

"So why do you think I'm involved?"

"C'mon, Deacon. Give me a little credit."

"Have you seen any sign of those two wet boys who tried to kill me Friday night?"

"Are you saying their bodies will turn up as well?"

"It was just a question."

"No sign of them."

"I guess you know Shields had a roommate."

"His name is Paul Givens, and we're looking for him now. Any information you'd like to volunteer would be highly appreciated."

"I know Givens was Shields's roommate. Other than that, I can't help you."

"This looks and sounds highly suspicious, Deacon. If the DA gets wind that you were even slightly involved in this--"

"You can't honestly believe I had anything to do with this murder. I'm a private eye, Neil. I look for people. I don't kill them."

"Give me some facts and maybe I'll reconsider."

"You want the name of my client, don't you?"

"It would help."

"You know I can't divulge that."

"What can you divulge?"

"I know Shields was involved in something-- well, something highly illegal."

"We already know that. The dump job kind of gave us a heads-up that he'd pissed off someone with serious anger issues."

"Givens was his roommate, and probably also involved. If I were a betting man, I'd say Givens is also dead, or has gone off to greener pastures."

"You know I could bring you in for this, don't you?"

"Yeah, but you won't."

"How can you be so sure?"

"I know you, Neil. Like most cops, you hate bad guys, and when they start offing one another, it's less work for you guys."

"I don't like it one bit when you withhold information. No cop does. We feel better when we have the answers. Helps us sleep better."

"Take a sleeping pill. Or have a relaxing drink before bedtime. I also hear occasional sex works wonders."

"You're pushing it, Deacon . . ."

"I'm not withholding anything. I've told you all I know. I was on a case, and I came across Shields during the investigation."

"How'd you come across him?"

"Like I said, he came up during my investigation."

"As I recall, you told me you had a feeling about him. Your words, not mine."

That was the scary thing about Neil. When you told him something, he never forgot, and used the information whenever he felt he needed it. He was like a hungry dog tearing a bone loose from its owner.

"As I recall, you were busy at the time."

"I'm always busy. You know that."

"Sure, I know that. That's why sometimes I tell you things just so you wouldn't hang up on me, like you often do."

"Now you're saying you told me you had a feeling about Shields just because you didn't want me to hang up on you?"

"You could say that."

"In other words, Shields wasn't involved in your investigation?"

"Just one of those leads that didn't go anywhere. Not where I wanted it to."

"You just stumbled across him."

"His name came up when my client mentioned something about a rare book that was stolen from his collection."

"Rare book?"

"One of those hardcover things printed a long time ago--"

"I *know* what a rare book is, Deacon."

"This one was printed in 1860." I sincerely hoped Neil wasn't a reader. I'd never seen evidence that he was. There were no paperbacks on any of his shelves. In fact, I didn't know any cop who actually read anything. "It was handed down through my client's family and worth a lot of money--"

"Deacon, it really pisses me off when you get me all stirred up and blow everything off later on, when the dust settles."

250

"Neil, I had nothing to do with Shields' murder. If I'd known about it, I would have definitely given you a heads-up."

Neil sighed, but I could tell he was still suspicious. "I guess I'll have to be satisfied with that."

"Just be happy Shields isn't still running around."

"What exactly *do* you know about him?"

"Just that he and Givens were dirty."

"I told you about Shields that same afternoon, when you asked me to pull his sheet. Besides, we just searched their apartment."

"What did you find?"

"Grass. Stolen guns. Drug money and enough cocaine to supply a hundred serious cokeheads for weeks."

"So they were dealers after all?"

"You . . . didn't know?"

"I honestly didn't." I decided to let Neil enjoy a little triumph for the moment. He didn't get to experience it very often.

"They were in it big-time. If Givens is also dead, I'd venture to say Orlando just lost two major suppliers."

"Sounds like OPD deserves a major slap on the back."

"This still doesn't get you off the hook."

"I figured as much."

"One of these days, this good luck streak of yours is bound to dry up."

"You keep telling me that. I just hope you're wrong."

"So am I." He hung up.

And I finished my breakfast.

***

That evening at Dante's *Ristorante*, Mike appeared at my booth just as I had a slug of Papa Joe's house wine.

She'd dressed up her image and looked ravishing in her black strapless evening dress and open-toed black pumps. Her hair hung loose, glistening in the candlelight. Her eyes also glistened. I could barely contain myself, and nearly spilled my drink.

"You all right, *paisano*?" Papa Joe blotted his mouth with a monogrammed towel. He wore a tan jacket and light-blue dress shirt opened at the neck, revealing a tuft of curly white chest hair. A light-blue silk handkerchief poked timidly out of his jacket pocket.

I had to clear my throat. It was important to keep cool despite Mike's grand entrance. Her amused grin wasn't helping. "Why do you ask?"

"You look like you just saw a ghost."

I coughed. Mike giggled. I tossed her a glare. "I'm all right. The wine . . . went down the wrong way."

Papa Joe nodded. "How's the shrimp?"

"Excellent."

"And the scallops?"

"Out of this world."

"Best food in the city."

"I won't argue."

"You need to come here more often. Whenever you solve an important case, mebbe."

"Can't afford it. I wouldn't be here tonight if you weren't paying."

"Don't give me that crap. You just made yourself a lot of cash for two days' work."

I couldn't take my eyes off Mike as she sat in front of our booth on her nonexistent chair, smiling at me. I wanted to tell her to stop smiling like that. Her smile was driving me crazy. It was filling my head with all sorts of nasty images. I wanted her to know what that dress was doing to me. But I knew better. She knew exactly what she was doing.

"What you keep looking at?"

"Um . . . the ladies here tonight are just as distracting as the food," I said, staring directly at her.

Papa Joe nodded. "They're all nice to look at, but when a woman's with someone else, it's *stupido,* getting yourself all worked up. *Capire?*"

"The ones here by themselves are definitely worth gawking at."

Papa Joe scanned the crowd. "I no see no unescorted ladies here."

"I guess my imagination's working overtime again."

Mike laughed.

"Rafaello, sometimes I worry about you. I'm sure your momma already knows. You've got what the shrinks nowadays would call issues."

"She's known that for years. And call me Deacon."

253

Papa Joe shook his head. "Deacon's so . . . *cold*."

"You call others by their last names."

"We're *paisanos*. You call me Papa Joe. . ."

"Deacon's a strong Irish name."

"You're more Italian than Irish. Mebbe I'll call you Raf."

"Roff?"

"Ever hear of Raf Vallone? The Italian movie star?"

"Yeah. He was in *Godfather*."

Papa Joe grunted. "That's *all* you know about one of your countrymen?"

"He's been dead a long time, hasn't he? And he wasn't, well, he wasn't *that* famous . . ."

"Where's your pride? Your sense of history? Vallone came from Calabria. That's where your momma's family's from. He was big and strong, played soccer. They used to compare him to Burt Lancaster. Remember *him*, don'tcha?"

"Well, yeah. The *Crimson Pirate*. I used to fall out of a lot of trees when I was a kid, and it was because of him."

Papa Joe blinked. "You . . . fell out of *trees*?"

"There were woods behind our house. I pretended the trees were the ship's masts. I was the Crimson Pirate and spent my summers climbing trees and swinging from the branches. A lot of those branches weren't exactly strong enough to swing from, and they just gave way beneath my weight. And other times, well, I missed altogether, and took a nosedive."

Papa Joe was nodding. "I understand now. Brain damage from falling on your head so much."

"My dad would've agreed with you."

"I would've liked seeing you as a little boy," Mike said.

"Mom thought I was as cute as a button. She didn't like me coming home all cut up, though."

"I wouldn't have liked it, either," she said. "But you're still cute as a button."

"Moms all think alike," Papa Joe said. "It's that umbilical cord bullshit. They no like it when it's cut." He shrugged. "Dads are more practical, see things better. I woulda cracked your butt, seeing you coming home bloodied and bruised all the time. It was undignified."

"And cracking my butt would've been dignified?"

"You needed to learn certain values."

"I was eight years old at the time!"

He had another sip of *vino*. "Still . . . values. They matter, *paisano*."

"I sure am glad you weren't my dad." I reached for my wine glass.

Papa Joe speared a fried oyster with his fork and nibbled on it. "So . . . whatta you gonna do with all that money? Buy a new car and get rid of that old wreck?"

"My car's a classic." I hated it when people dissed my ride.

"I like it," Mike said, smiling.

"It's old," Papa Joe said. "Tired. Seen better days. Like me."

"It's a chick magnet."

"You're sick. Your momma, she should worry about you."

"She does. All the time."

"She needs comforting."

"You want to shack up with my *mother*?"

Papa Joe's eyes blazed. "*Idiota*. You need your mouth washed out with soap."

"Now you sound like one of my aunts."

"Your aunt, she sounds bright."

"Want to meet her?"

Papa Joe sighed tiredly and massaged his temples. "Like I said, you're sick. *Malato*. It's the Irish in you."

"It was the Italian in me that got your organization back."

"And me," Mike said.

"Yes. And you."

"Howzat?"

I smiled at Mike. "Just thinking aloud."

"*Si*." Papa Joe nodded. "Sick, Raf. Very sick."

"I like Raf, too," Mike said.

When Mike said it, it sounded cool.

"Who am I to argue with such a beautiful lady?"

"Brain damage, definitely. From falling on your head so much." Papa Joe shook his head and poured more *vino* into our glasses.

THE END

OTHER BOOKS BY DAVID BERARDELLI

Titles available through:
Fiction4All

www.ingramcontent.com/pod-product-compliance
Lightning Source LLC
Chambersburg PA
CBHW010748250626
47155CB00010B/3543